The Upside of Love

Sandi Lynn

Cover Design by Cover It Designs

Models: Pato Margetic & Mikeala Galli-Model

Photographer Lindee Robinson @ Lindee Robinson Photography

Photo Image/Guitar D7INAMI7S/Shutterstock

Editing by B.Z. Hercules

Table of Contents

Chapter 1

Lily

"Have I told you how much I love you, Luke Matthews?" I asked as I ran my hand across his chest.

"You have, babe, and I don't ever want you to stop telling me."

I lifted my head from his chest and kissed his lips – the lips that devoured every inch of my skin last night from head to toe. The lips that made me warm when I was cold, and the lips that gave me the security I desperately needed.

It had been two months since Sam's and Gretchen's accident. Gretchen's leg was healing nicely and Sam waited on her hand and foot, practically never leaving her side. Luke pretty much moved into my apartment, since Sam moved Gretchen into his. Lucky was staying with Giselle at her place because his apartment building had a flood and it was being renovated. Their relationship was still weird. Even though Giselle was pregnant with Lucky's kid, it didn't stop the two of them from seeing other people. It was awkward when one of them would bring the other out with us.

"I guess I should get up and head over to the bar," Luke sighed.

I tightened my arm around him because I didn't want to move. "No," I said.

"What do you mean?" Luke laughed.

"I think we should stay in bed all day and do nothing but have wild sex." I smiled as my hand traveled down to his hard cock.

"You sure know how to turn me on, babe," he said as he rolled me over and hovered over me. "I have to go to the bar. You have to edit those photos for Mrs. Braxton, and we have a lunch date with Charley today." He smiled as he took down my panties.

"You're right. But, promise me we'll schedule a day when we can just stay in bed all day and not worry about the outside world."

"You got it." He smiled as he plunged his finger inside me. "Now, give me your lips and shush. I'm going to make sweet love to you."

After a sweet round of lovemaking, Luke took a shower and I made a pot of coffee. As I waited for it to finish brewing, I stared out my window at the perfectly blue sky and the sun that was shining brightly into my living room. Settling in Santa Monica was the best decision I ever made. Lost in my thoughts, I felt strong arms wrap around me. I tilted my head back and looked up at Luke's smiling face.

"What are you doing?" he asked.

"Just admiring the beauty of the day."

He was wearing only jeans and his hair was still soaking wet. He was the sexiest man alive, as far as I was concerned, and I couldn't seem to get enough of him.

"Well, I'm admiring the beauty in front of me." He bent down and softly kissed my neck.

I giggled. "You sure have a way with words, Mr. Matthews."

"And you have a way with those lips." He smiled as he kissed me again.

Luke walked to the coffee pot, poured a cup of coffee, and sat down at the table.

"Do you want me to make you breakfast?" I asked.

"Nah, I'm good, babe. I'll grab something at the bar."

There was a knock at the door and Sam's boisterous voice came through loud and clear. "Dude, are you up? Are you decent?"

Luke sighed as he got up from his chair and opened the door.

"Morning, Sam. Morning, Gretchen."

I smiled as my best friends walked into the apartment. I immediately grabbed two cups and poured coffee in them.

"Sit down," I said to Gretchen and I lightly took hold of her arm and led her to the table.

"Thanks, Lily." She smiled.

"Have you talked to Giselle?" I asked.

"Yeah. She said that she and Lucky were going furniture shopping for the baby's room."

"For both places?" Luke asked.

"I'm not sure. She didn't say and I know his apartment still isn't ready. To be honest, I think she likes having him around."

"They're weird." I laughed.

Luke got up from the table. "Okay, friends. It's been fun seeing you, but I have to finish getting dressed and head over to the bar. Maddie and I have some liquor orders to go over."

"We playing tonight?" Sam asked.

"Yeah. I already talked to Lucky and he said that he and Giselle will be there. I'm also interviewing new bands to play on the weekends after we play our gig. I want Lily to play and she won't," he said as he pouted.

"Get over it, Matthews." I winked.

Luke headed to the bedroom to get ready, and Sam and Gretchen got up to leave. "I can't wait to get this cast off today. So, when you see me tonight, I'll be strutting in."

I laughed as I hugged her.

"I can't wait to finally make love to her without that cast getting in the way." Sam smiled.

"Just keep it down," Luke yelled from the bedroom.

"Paybacks, bro. Paybacks." He laughed.

****

Since I couldn't get another teaching job right away, I decided to make photography my full-time work. I mostly just worked out of my apartment, but I wanted to rent a small space and turn it into a studio. It was something that I'd thought about over the past couple of months and Luke was extremely supportive. He told me that I needed to follow my dreams and just go for it like he did with the bar. I did a photo shoot with Rory Braxton and her twin girls. It was a surprise gift for her husband's birthday. I photographed them at the beach and then Rory wanted some sexy pictures for Ian. I brought her back to the apartment once I set it up with the backdrop. I had never photographed sexy pictures like the ones I did for her and I was nervous at first. But after seeing the photographs, I knew she'd be more than pleased. I met Rory through Giselle. Rory's husband's best friend, Adalynn, owned *Prim* magazine, for which Giselle did a lot of modeling. When she overheard Rory and Adalynn talking about finding a female photographer, she instantly thought of me. Since the pictures that Rory wanted for Ian were of her practically naked and very seductive, she thought it would be best to have a female photograph her, so as not to upset her husband.

As I was sitting at my computer, editing the photos, Luke walked up and gave me a kiss.

"Bye, babe. Have fun today and I'll see you later at the bar for lunch with Charley."

"Bye, baby." I smiled.

I looked at the photos of Ashley and Ariel Braxton and smiled as I envisioned a family like Rory's and Ian's one day. I picked up my phone from the desk and called Rory.

"Hello," she answered.

"Hi, Rory. It's Lily. Your pictures will be ready by tonight, so I was hoping we could meet for lunch tomorrow and I can show you the final shots."

"Excellent, Lily. Tomorrow will be perfect. If you're in the mood for Mexican food, we can meet at the Border Grill, say around noon?"

"Sounds great, Rory. I'll see you tomorrow."

As I was editing the photos, one popped up of Luke. I smiled as I ran my fingers across his perfect six pack on the screen. It was one of him lying on the bed in only a pair of unbuttoned jeans. His arm was behind his head and he was looking out the window.

I was the luckiest girl alive to be loved by him and my life was perfect. More perfect than I had ever dreamed it would be.

Chapter 2

Luke

I walked into the bar and saw Adam talking to Maddie. So far, he had kept his word and he was turning his life around. He attended UCLA like he said he would, and he also worked full-time in the IT department at Rocket Corp. He saw Charley and Maddie as much as he could and I could tell that Maddie was falling in love with him again. Actually, she had always loved him. I thought he should make computers his career, but he wanted to be a counselor for drug and alcohol abuse. As long as he kept true to his word about changing, I was cool with him. Charley loved having him around and so close. And if she was happy, that was all that mattered.

"Hey, you two," I said as I walked over to the bar.

"Hey, man," Adam replied.

Maddie looked at me and smiled. "Charley is really looking forward to having lunch with you and Lily today."

"Yeah, we are too. We better go over the liquor order before she gets here."

Adam gave Maddie a kiss goodbye and told me he'd see me later. I took out the invoice with the liquor order on it and Maddie and I started to check the boxes.

"Can I ask what the two of you were talking about?"

"Not really, but I'll tell you anyway," she said. "He wants to take Charley and me to Disneyland this weekend. Just the three of us, like a family."

"How do you feel about that?" I asked.

"I love him, Luke. I always have. I want us to be a family."

"Please tell me that he's not spending the night at your place. I don't want Charley to get her hopes up."

"He's not," she said as she looked at the invoice.

"Go to Disneyland and be a family." I smiled as I kissed her cheek. "Charley will love it."

As I was pulling the liquor bottles out of the boxes, my phone buzzed in my pocket. I pulled it out and there was a text message from a number I didn't recognize.

"Hi, Uncle Luke. It's me, Charley. Hehe."

I looked at my sister and showed her my phone. "What the hell is this?"

"We bought Charley a cell phone last night and, before you say anything, she's only allowed to text me, Adam, you, Lily, and Mom and Dad. It's for emergency purposes only."

"Really, Maddie? You don't think she's a little young to be responsible for a cell phone?"

She rolled her eyes. "All the kids her age have them and I like knowing that I can get a hold of her any time I want."

"So if all the kids her age had horses, you'd go out and buy her a horse?"

She twisted her face and looked up at the ceiling. "Yeah, I would. I love horses." She smiled. "Relax, Uncle Luke; it'll be fine."

"Don't come crying to me if she goes over her minutes and you're paying a small fortune for your bill."

"She won't. Now text her back." She winked.

"Awesome, peanut. I'll see you for lunch and you can show me your new phone."

"Okay."

Maddie and I finished putting the liquor away and I went to my office. I had so much paperwork to catch up on. I was finding it difficult to do everything on my own. Sure, Maddie helped, but she tended bar with Candi. Neither one of them were suited for secretarial work. I was beginning to think that I needed to hire someone part-time. Maybe to come in to the bar three times a week and do the paperwork and help with the books. I got up from my chair and just as I opened the door, my two beautiful girls were standing there.

"Why, hello there, beautiful ladies." I smiled.

"Uncle Luke!" Charley exclaimed as she threw her arms around my waist.

"Hi, Charley. Hey, babe." I smiled as I leaned over and kissed Lily on the cheek. "Did you get those photos done?"

"I sure did and I'm meeting Rory tomorrow for lunch to show her."

"Great. Now let's go eat. I'm starving," I said.

"You should have let me make you breakfast." Lily smiled.

"If I recall, I had a great breakfast this morning." I winked.

We walked out of the bar and Lily threw me the keys to her Explorer. "Where do you want to go eat?"

"At the beach." Charley smiled.

"The beach? We can't have lunch at the beach."

"Sure we can, Uncle Luke. We can stop and get some sandwiches to go and then take them to the beach. Lily has a blanket back here."

"Smart little girl." Lily smiled as she looked at me.

"Okay, then; the beach it is."

****

We spread out the blanket and took our sandwiches out of the bag. "One ham and cheese on white for you," I said as I handed Charley her sandwich. "And one tuna on whole wheat for you, babe."

"Thank you."

It was a beautiful day to spend at the beach. I just wished we could have spent the entire day there. But there was way too much to get done at the bar. As soon as we finished our lunch, Charley went and played by the shoreline. She loved the way the waves crashed into her feet. I leaned over and pushed Lily's hair behind her ear. She placed her hand on mine and interlaced our fingers.

"What's wrong? I can tell something's bothering you," she said.

I sighed. "I think I need to hire a secretary or an assistant to handle all the paperwork at the bar. It's becoming too much to do on my own."

She softly smiled at me as she brought my hand up to her lips. "Then hire someone. If you need the help, then just do it. I don't want to see you so stressed out."

"Maybe I will." I smiled as I leaned in and kissed her seductively on her lips.

"Hey, no kissing in public." Charley smiled.

"Is that so, little girl?" I laughed as I grabbed her and tickled her in the sand.

We grabbed the blanket, shook it out, and Lily dropped me off at the bar. "Bye, babe. I'll see you later. Ask Sam to give you a ride to the bar tonight and we can ride home on my bike."

"Aren't you coming home to change?" she asked with disappointment.

"I have so much paperwork to catch up on and I want to get a jump on it. Does that make you mad?"

"No. I'll call Sam and ask him." She smiled.

I leaned over and gave her a kiss and then kissed Charley on the cheek. I went straight to my office and shut the door. I didn't want to be disturbed until the gang arrived later.

****

"Is it safe to come in?" Lily asked as she poked her head through the door.

I looked up from what I was doing and smiled. "Of course it is, babe. Get in here."

She walked in and sat down on my lap, wrapping her arms around my neck and planting a big kiss on my lips.

"I missed you," she said.

"I missed you too."

"Have you even made a dent in any of this?"

"Some. Not much. I did place an ad in the paper for help. It runs tomorrow, so keep your fingers crossed that people respond. Is everyone here?"

"Everyone with the exception of Giselle and Lucky. I called them and they're on their way."

She got up from my lap and I got up from my chair. We walked out into the bar together and I saw Gretchen and Sam standing, talking to Candi.

"Look at you." I smiled as I kissed Gretchen. "No more cast. How does it feel?"

"I'm still trying to get used to it." She laughed.

"You look great, Gretchen," I told her.

"Thanks, Luke."

"Sammy, let's get the equipment set up. Why isn't Lucky here yet?"

"Keep your panties on, dude. I'm here." Lucky smiled as he held out his arms.

The three of us went and set up the stage. I looked across the bar at Lily as she stood there, talking to our friends. I never thought I could love again since Callie. But Lily changed all that for me. She breathed life into me again, and now, every breath I took was for her.

Chapter 3

Lily

I was nervous to show Rory the pictures. I knew I shouldn't be because they turned out so great, but I was always nervous when it came to showing my work. I put the photos in the Explorer and drove to the Border Grill. When I arrived, Rory was already sitting down in a booth, waiting for me.

"Hi, Lily." She smiled as she got up and hugged me.

"Hi, Rory."

"I took the liberty of ordering you a margarita. I hope that's okay."

"Of course. I love margaritas." I smiled.

I sat down and set the box of photos on the table.

"So, I'm dying to see my pictures," she said.

I took the lid off the box and pulled out the pictures of her and the girls first. I displayed them nicely on the table in front of her. She looked at them and then at me.

"These are absolutely gorgeous! Oh, Lily, these are going to look wonderful in my house."

"I'm glad you like them."

"I don't like them. I love them!" she exclaimed. "And?" she said with a smile.

I took out the photos that she had made for Ian. "You might want to keep these down in your seat while you look at them." I laughed.

"Right." She laughed with me.

She didn't say anything at first. She just kept staring at the half-naked pictures of herself. Finally, she looked at me with a tear in her eye.

"These pictures are amazing. You have captured my heart and soul and Ian is going to love them. In fact, he may have a heart attack." She smiled.

"Let's hope that doesn't happen." I laughed.

"Can you put all of the photos of me in a hard-bound photo album? And, if possible, I would like Ian's name engraved on it. No, actually, I want it to say: *To the love of my life, my husband, best friend, and lover.*"

"Of course I can. Don't worry, Rory. I'll take care of it."

She reached over and grabbed my hand. You are an amazing photographer and I'm so happy Giselle introduced me to you."

"Thank you. I'm thrilled that you had the confidence in me to hire me to photograph you and your beautiful girls."

We placed our order with the waitress and we continued to talk while sipping on margaritas. "Have you thought about opening up a studio?" she asked.

"I have. I've been thinking about it for the past couple of months, but I wouldn't know where to start looking."

She picked up her glass and took a sip of her drink. "My husband, Ian, is in real estate development and he owns a small strip mall right down the road from here. I happen to know that there's a shop for rent because it's right next door to the hair salon where I get my hair done. It's the perfect location and it gets a lot of traffic. I think it would make a great photography studio. If you want, I can call Ian and tell him to meet us there after lunch."

I sat there, blown away at this amazing opportunity that Rory was giving me. "That would be great, Rory. Thank you." I smiled.

She reached into her purse and pulled out her phone. She called her husband and he said that he could meet us there in about a half hour.

"If he asks how we met, we'll just tell him we met through Giselle at *Prim* and we got to talking. I don't want him to know that you photographed me and the girls."

"No worries. Your secret is safe with me."

Rory took care of the bill, even though I tried to fight her on it, and I followed her to the strip mall. Ian was waiting for us inside the shop. As we walked in, he turned around, and I couldn't help but notice how extremely handsome he was.

"Ian, this is my new friend, Lily Gilmore. She's the one who is looking to open up a photography studio."

"It's very nice to meet you, Lily. I'm Ian Braxton." He smiled as he held out his hand.

"Thank you for coming out here on such short notice, Mr. Braxton."

"Please, call me Ian, and it's no problem at all."

I smiled as he showed me around the shop. Instantly, I could envision me opening up a studio here. It was the perfect size and perfect location. "I love it, Ian. I can totally see me working out of this space."

"Great. Why don't you have dinner with Rory and me at our house tonight, and I'll draw up the contract and go over the specifics with you? Bring your husband along."

"I'm not married, but I do have a boyfriend," I said.

"Perfect. Bring him along and the four of us can have a nice dinner and talk. I better get going. "Bye, sweetheart," he said as he kissed his wife. "I'll call Charles and tell him about dinner. It was great to meet you, Lily, and I look forward to seeing you and—"

"Luke."

"You and Luke tonight." He smiled as he shook my hand.

We walked out of the store and he climbed in his limo and pulled away. I looked over at Rory, who was smiling from ear to ear.

"I told you this would be perfect," she said.

"Thank you, Rory. You have no idea how much this means to me," I said as I hugged her.

"No problem. You're an incredible photographer and you should have your own studio. I'll see you tonight. Around seven?"

"Seven is great. Bye, Rory."

I got into my Explorer and called Luke.

"Hey, babe. What's up?" he answered.

"Please tell me you can get off early tonight."

"Why? What's going on?"

I was so excited to tell him the news. "We are having dinner tonight with the Braxton's at their home."

"Okay. Why?"

"Because I found the perfect place to open up a studio and it just so happens that Mr. Ian Braxton owns it."

"Ah, perfect. Okay. Are you at the place now?"

"Yeah. I was just leaving."

"Give me the address, stay put, and I'll be there quick. I want to see it."

"Okay, baby. I'll wait for you."

I texted him the address and sat in the truck and waited for him. About ten minutes later, he rode up on his motorcycle. I got out of my truck and wrapped my arms around him.

"Thank you for coming."

"Anything for you, babe. Show me the shop."

"It's this one right here," I said as I pointed to the empty shop that sat in the middle of the strip mall.

He looked through the window and then looked around at the area. "I think this would be a great place for you to start. Great space, great location, great shops around. "Good choice, babe." He smiled as he kissed me. He looked at his watch and then at me. "I think I'll come home for the day. I need to make sweet love to you and then take a shower." He smiled.

"Really?" I asked with excitement.

"Yep. I've been thinking about you all day long and how bad I want to take you to bed."

"We just did it this morning." I giggled.

"Exactly, and it was so magical that I want more. You know I can never get enough of you, babe."

"I can never get enough of you either. Let's go."

Luke hopped on his bike and took off and I followed behind. As soon as we pulled into the parking lot of the apartments, Luke got off his bike and opened my driver's side door. He reached in and smashed his mouth against mine. I turned my body around and wrapped my legs tightly around his waist as he picked me up and carried me to the building. His kiss was forceful and loving. I ran my fingers through his hair as he put me up against the wall, right outside the building. As he was devouring my mouth and then my neck, I reached in his pants pocket and took out his keys. He held me up against the wall with one hand as the other inserted the key to the building and he unlocked the door. I started to giggle because he couldn't open it.

"For God's sake. Can't the two of you wait until you get inside your apartment?" Sam said as he opened the door and held it for us.

"No time, bro. I've been thinking about this all day," Luke said as he kissed me.

"Here, let me open your door for you," Sam said as he rolled his eyes.

He took the keys and opened my apartment door. "There you go. Have fun, you two."

Luke carried me straight to the bedroom and we both fell on the bed. He broke our kiss, stood up, and lifted his shirt over his head. While he unbuttoned his jeans and took them down, I sat up and got undressed, throwing my clothes on the floor.

"Don't take your bra off yet, babe. I want to do it." He smiled.

I sat there as he stood in front of me, naked, looking like a god. He leaned over and unhooked my bra from the back while he took down each strap slowly.

"God, I'll never get tired of looking at you. You are more and more beautiful every day," he said as his lips hovered over mine.

He lifted my hips and took down my thong. His mouth consumed every inch of my body before he plunged two fingers inside me, making sure I was ready for him.

"Babe, you're so wet. God, I need you now."

I spread my legs wide open for him as he hovered over me and began to thrust in and out of me. I was so aroused by him, it felt like I was already going to come. His moans were deep and sensual as he moved fluidly inside me. I wrapped my legs around his waist as he kneaded my breast. My moans were growing louder by the minute as I felt him swell inside me. His finger reached my clit and began making small circles around it, sending me over the edge.

"That's it, babe. I know you're about to come. Fucking come for me because I can't hold back anymore."

My legs tightened as the orgasm overtook my body. Luke moaned as he pushed himself deeper inside me, filling me with every last drop of pleasure he had inside him. As he collapsed on top of me, we tried to catch our breath.

"I love you, Lily."

I smiled as I pressed my lips against his neck. "I love you too."

Once our breathing returned to normal, Luke sat up and smiled at me. "Are you ready for round two in the shower?"

"I am if you are."

He looked down between his legs. "What do you think that means?" He winked.

****

"Come in. It's good to see you again, Lily." Ian smiled as he kissed my cheek.

"Ian, this is my boyfriend, Luke Matthews," I said as they shook hands.

"Rory will be down in a minute. Please, come sit down. Luke, you look like a beer kind of guy."

Luke chuckled. "I am."

"I have some imported beer I'd like you to try."

"I would love to," he said.

Ian looked at me and smiled. "Lily, you're a red wine type of girl."

"That's right, Ian. I am."

Rory walked into the room and we lightly hugged. I introduced her to Luke and the four of us went and sat down on the patio for dinner. We talked, laughed, and ate the wonderful food that Charles prepared for us. Ian kept staring at me from across the table. To be honest, it was making me really uncomfortable and I thought he could tell.

"I apologize for staring at you, Lily. But you seem very familiar to me and I can't put my finger on it."

Luke looked at me and smiled. Then he turned his attention to Ian. "You probably know her as the daughter of Johnny Gilmore."

Ian immediately snapped his fingers. "That's it! I knew your name was familiar. Your father was a brilliant musician. I'm so sorry about his death."

"Thank you, Ian."

"You know, his picture is hanging on the wall at the Piano Bar. Rory's father is the owner."

"Wait," Luke interrupted. "Jimmy O'Rourke is your dad?" he asked as he looked at Rory.

"Yes, he is." Rory smiled. "Do you know him?"

"Yeah. I've known him for years. He and Bernie go way back. He used to come into Bernie's bar all the time. I didn't know he had a daughter."

My head was going back and forth, listening to their conversation.

"It's a long story," Ian said.

"Wow, what a small world."

After we finished our dinner, Ian and I got up and went into his office to go over and sign the rental contract. As he was going over the contract, Ariel and Ashley came running in. They stopped when they saw me.

"That's the lady who took our picture," Ashley said.

Ariel walked up to me and placed her hand on my cheek. "Hi again." She smiled.

Ian looked at me strangely. "Girls, it's way past your bedtime. Now give Daddy kisses and head to your rooms. I'll be up in a few minutes to tuck you in."

"Okay, Daddy." They giggled as they kissed his cheeks.

Ariel turned to me. "Will you take our picture again?"

"I'd be happy to." I smiled.

They ran out the door, shutting it behind them, and Ian cocked his head. Before he could say anything, I spoke first.

"Listen, Rory wanted this to be a huge surprise for you, so please don't let her know that you know. It will really upset her."

"It's for my birthday, isn't it?" he asked.

I nodded my head.

"I won't say a word about it. I promise."

"Your girls are beautiful." I smiled.

"They are the loves of my life. All three of them."

I sat there thinking what an incredible man Ian Braxton was and how much he loved Rory. I could see it in his eyes every time she walked in the room. I signed the last piece of paper and Ian smiled at me as he held out his hand.

"Congratulations, Lily."

"Thanks, Ian. Thank you for everything."

"You're quite welcome. Once you get your studio set up, I'd love to come see it."

I smiled and we walked back to the patio where Luke and Rory were. We drank a couple more glasses of wine and then headed home.

Chapter 4

Luke

I threw my keys on the counter as soon as we walked into the apartment. Lily headed straight for the bathroom and I went into the bedroom. As soon as I climbed in bed, I checked my email and was surprised when I saw I had over twenty responses to my help wanted ad.

"Lily, hurry up, babe."

She walked into the bedroom in nothing but her bra and panties with her hair piled on top of her head.

"Damn, woman. You're killing me." I smiled as I watched her take off her bra and slip on the nightshirt she pulled from the drawer.

"Behave yourself, Mr. Matthews," she said as she climbed in beside me.

"Look, babe. Look at all these responses to my ad."

"That's great. Are you going to start interviewing soon?"

"Yep. I'll start setting them up tomorrow morning."

I set down my phone and wrapped my arms around her, pulling her close to me and inhaling her scent as she snuggled against my chest.

"I loved you taking a half of day off from the bar and spending it with me. When I open up the studio, I'm afraid things are going to get so busy that we won't have time for each other anymore."

"Aw, babe. Don't say that. We will always have time for each other. We'll make time. Don't worry about that. Remember, no matter how crazy life gets, there's always time for Love In Between."

She smiled as she looked up at me. "That's how you came up with the name for your band."

"Yeah. That's right," I said as I kissed her head.

"I love you, Luke. Good night."

"I love you more, Lily. Good night, babe."

****

I awoke to the aroma of coffee going up my nose. I opened one eye and saw Lily sitting over me, holding a cup of coffee in my face.

"Morning," I said as I rubbed my eyes.

"Good morning. Time to get up, sleepy head. You have interviews to schedule and I have a shop to put together."

I took the mug from her and sat up. "Okay. Okay. I'm up. But I refuse to get out of this bed until my beautiful girlfriend gives me a kiss."

"I think that can be arranged." She smiled as she leaned in and kissed me.

She jumped up from the bed and pulled a sundress out of the closet. "I'm so excited. I sent Gretchen and Giselle a text and told them that I'm taking them somewhere today. I'm going to surprise them and take them to the shop. They're going to flip!" she squealed.

Seeing the excitement pour out from Lily was amazing. I was so happy that she was finally going to live her life as a photographer with her own studio. I wanted nothing more than for her to be happy. My phone buzzed and there was a text message from Lucky.

"Dude, fuck me, man. Giselle is so hormonal she's driving me nuts. One minute we're laughing together and the next she's screaming at me."

I chuckled. *"Pamper her and just take it. She's the mother of your child. Remember that."*

"Somehow I knew you'd say something like that."

"It seems Giselle is being overly hormonal with Lucky." I laughed.

"She's overly hormonal when she's *not* pregnant." Lily smiled.

I got out of bed and jumped into the shower. When I finished, Lily was standing in the doorway of the bathroom, staring at me.

"You want some of this?" I smiled.

"Yes, but later. I need to lay down some rules for you when interviewing these women who applied to be your assistant."

"Oh, really? And what rules would that be?" I asked with a smirk as I dried off.

"They must not be attractive. They must be fully clothed and they must have the personality of a doormat. Actually, a lesbian would be perfect."

I walked over to her and placed my hands on her hips. "Are you really worried, babe?"

"I'm a woman and sometimes a woman can be insecure when it comes to other women working with the man she loves."

"Please, Lily, you know me better than that," I said as I kissed her forehead.

"It's not you I don't trust, it's the other women. I mean, look at you. You are an incredibly sexy man and any woman would be stupid not to try and get her hooks into you. I deal with it every time we go out."

"I love you and only you, babe. You know that. Now stop with the nonsense. But I will keep your rules in mind." I winked.

"Thank you, baby. Okay, I'm off to the studio! I love you." She smiled as she kissed me goodbye.

"I love you too, Lil. Have fun and I'll see you later."

****

When I arrived at the bar, Lucky was there, doing some wiring on the stage.

"Dude, when are the chicks coming? I think I need to sit in on the interviews with you so you can make the right choice."

"You are not sitting in on the interviews and you're going to be a father."

"So. What's your point?"

"Focus on your kid."

"Man, Giselle is busting my balls. You know, I love her, but then I hate her. Do you know what I mean?"

"Actually, I don't," I said as I walked to my office.

"What's going on with you?" Lucky asked.

"Nothing. It's just Lily is worried about who I'll hire for my assistant."

"Why would she be worried? You're...you." He laughed.

"Exactly, and I told her that."

"Chicks are weird. It's probably just a hormone thing like Giselle."

"Lily's not pregnant."

"No, not yet anyway!" He winked.

As I was about to kick him out of my office, there was a brunette in standing in the doorway.

"Well, hello, Angel. How may I help you?" Lucky smiled as he took her hand and lightly kissed it.

"I have an interview with the owner, Luke."

"Well, that would be—"

"Me," I said as I stepped from behind my desk. "I'm Luke Matthews."

"Hi, Mr. Matthews. My name is Cody Chase."

"Cody, I love that name and it's so you." Lucky smiled.

"Lucky, get the hell out of here."

"I'm going. I'm going," he said. "Maybe Cody and I can chat later." He smiled.

I shut the door and shook my head. "Ignore my friend. He has way too much testosterone."

She giggled and sat down in the chair across from me.

The interview went good and she was very qualified for the job, but I had others I had to interview today and tomorrow, so I told her that I'd get back with her either way. After I walked Cody to the door, I took a seat at the bar.

"How was she?" Maddie asked.

"She was good. Very qualified. I liked her. She's a good candidate."

"She's very pretty," Maddie said as she wiped a glass.

"I didn't notice."

"Good answer." She smiled.

"The next girl should be here in about five minutes. Just send her to my office."

"Will do, boss."

Chapter 5

Lily

I couldn't wait to show Giselle and Gretchen the studio. It was something I'd talked about for a long time. They had no clue about any of this. I wanted it to be a total surprise. Gretchen and I watched as Giselle waddled her way to the car. I couldn't help but smile at her because she looked so damn cute and she was the last person that I'd thought would have a baby.

"So, where are you taking us?" she asked as she climbed into the car.

"It's a surprise. How are you feeling?"

"Besides fat and bloated, I'm feeling pretty good. Lucky and I have an ultrasound scheduled for tomorrow. We're going to find out the sex of the baby."

"That's awesome! You better call me the second you find out."

"Nope, actually, I'm having all of you over tomorrow night for dinner and then you'll find out." Giselle smiled.

"Hopefully, Luke can make it. He's been so buried at the bar."

I pulled in the parking lot and into the space right in front of the studio.

"Follow me, ladies." I smiled as I unlocked the door.

"Lily, what is this?" Gretchen asked.

"Welcome to A Day In The Life Photography Studio."

"What?! Oh my God!" the both of them exclaimed.

"This is amazing, Lily. Congratulations!" Giselle said as she hugged me.

"I can't believe it. You finally have your own studio and Luke has his bar. You two are so perfect and you're going to have an incredible future," Gretchen said as she hugged me.

"Yeah. Life is really good." I smiled. I would have to look into hiring a contractor to come in and fix up the inside. I have all kinds of equipment I need to buy. Oh my God, I think I'm freaking out."

Giselle and Gretchen laughed. "Don't stress, and take it one day at a time. We'll help you as much as we can. Plus, you have that handsome boyfriend of yours to help," Giselle replied.

"Luke is so busy with the bar that he needs to hire an assistant. I laid down the ground rules this morning about who he can and can't hire."

"Well, if he hires some hottie, then you'll have to do the same because you're going to need help here."

"Very true." I smiled.

"I may have the name of a contractor for you. He's the boyfriend of Sierra Adams over at Adams Advertising, the agency that *Prim* uses to help with the magazine."

"Perfect!" I smiled.

"I'll text you his number later. Now, can we go grab some lunch? This little one is starving," Giselle said as she rubbed her tummy.

Giselle craved Mexican food. In fact, she ate it every day. We sat down in the booth and I pulled out my phone and sent Luke a text message.

"Hi, baby. How did your interviews go?"

"Hi, babe. They went really good. What are you doing?"

"I'm having lunch with Giselle and Gretchen. I hope they were ugly?"

"They were smokin hot, babe. I can't help it."

"Very funny. You'll pay for that when you get home."

"I know. That's why I said it."

"Bye."

"Bye."

After we placed our order, I asked Giselle about Lucky.

"So what's going on with you and Lucky?"

"What do you mean? He's my baby daddy and that's about it. We've been fighting a lot. Like an old married couple."

"I walked in on them the other day having sex on the couch," Gretchen said as she bit into a chip.

"When's he moving out?"

"As soon as his place is ready. They said probably about another month."

"Do you want him to leave? I mean, you are going to need help with the baby."

"He's messy and he doesn't listen. He leaves the toilet seat up and I almost fell in the other night when I went to go pee because it was dark. He leaves his dishes in the sink and his socks in every room in the house. His shoes are always in the middle of the floor and he leaves glass rings on my tables."

Gretchen and I sat there laughing. We both silently thanked God that Sam and Luke weren't like that.

"Well, then I guess it's time for him to leave." I smiled.

"I love him but then I hate him. He's very immature. Anyway, dinner is at seven tomorrow night."

"We will be there." I smiled.

****

I picked up Charley from school because Maddie was tied up at the bar and Adam was in class. As much as I missed teaching, my passion was photography.

"Hey, baby girl." I smiled as Charley climbed into the Explorer.

"Hi, Lily. Guess what?"

"What?"

"I got Student of the Week!" She smiled as she showed me her award.

"Fantastic, Charley! Give me a high five. Wait until your mom and Uncle Luke find out."

"Can we go for ice cream?" she asked.

"We sure can. Let's go."

I drove us to the ice cream parlor and, when I opened the door, Charley walked through and I stopped. I couldn't shake the feeling that someone was following or watching me. After looking around and seeing nothing and no one, I joined Charley at the counter and we picked out what kind of ice cream we were going to have. As we were eating our ice cream, I had an idea.

"Let's Face Time Uncle Luke and show him what we're doing."

"Yeah! He'll be so jealous."

I pulled out my phone and proceeded to Face Time him. He answered.

"Hey, babe. What are you doing?" He laughed.

"Charley and I are sitting in the ice cream parlor having ice cream and we wanted to show you."

"Hey, peanut!" Luke said as Charley appeared on the screen.

"Hi, Uncle Luke. Look; I got your favorite ice cream." She laughed as she showed him her cone.

"No fair. I want some."

"You can't because you're not here." Charley smiled.

"You two have all the fun."

"I know you're busy. So I'll see you later."

"I love you, babe."

"I love you too." I smiled as I kissed the screen.

"That's gross," Charley said. "My mom and dad are always kissing on the couch. Yuck!"

"Someday, when you're older, you'll want to kiss the boy you're in love with," I said.

"No way. I don't want to get cooties. My mom said that all boys have cooties."

I laughed as I tapped her on the nose. Once we finished, I took Charley back to my apartment and she did homework while I went into the bedroom. I looked at the guitar sitting in the corner and picked it up. I began strumming the chords.

"Lily," Charley said as she stood in the doorway.

"Yeah, baby."

"Will you teach me how to play?"

"Of course I will. Come here," I said as I held out my hand.

She walked over to me with a smile on her face and sat down next to me. I set the guitar in her lap and positioned her fingers on the strings to form a D chord. As she strummed, I adjusted her fingers so she was playing correctly. I had flashbacks of my father sitting on the edge of his bed, teaching me.

"What's going on in here?" Luke smiled as he stood in the doorway.

"I'm teaching Charley a few chords."

"Look, Uncle Luke, I'm playing!" she exclaimed as she strummed the chords.

"I see that, peanut, and I'm jealous. You never asked me to teach you to play."

"You can teach me too." She smiled.

I got up from the bed and gave Luke a kiss.

"How did it go at the studio?" he asked.

"It went well. Giselle and Gretchen loved it, and they're excited for me. Giselle has the name of a contractor she's giving me to get in contact with."

"Good. Maddie should be here shortly. She and Adam are taking Charley out to dinner."

"What are we doing for dinner? Do you want to stay in and cook?" I asked.

Luke softly kissed my head. "That sounds like a plan. Do we have anything here?"

I laughed. "No. We'd have to go to the store and buy something."

"Then I think it sounds like a take-out kind of night." He smiled.

Maddie arrived a few moments later to pick up Charley. She didn't want to leave because she wanted to practice playing the one chord I taught her.

"Have a great dinner, Charley." I smiled as I kissed her on the cheek. "You can come over and practice anytime you want."

"Thanks, Lily. I love you." She smiled as she hugged me.

"I love you too, baby."

She kissed Luke goodbye and, as the door shut, I had a thought.

"We need to buy Charley her own guitar," I said.

"I was thinking that too. I have an older guitar I can give her to practice on and if she becomes really serious about playing, then we can buy her one."

"That's a good idea." I smiled as I wrapped my arms around him.

Chapter 6

Luke

Lily and I sat in bed and shared cartons of Chinese food. It had been a while since we just relaxed and did nothing.

"Are you going to tell me about the girls or what?" she asked.

"What girls?" I smiled as I fed her a piece of pork from my chopsticks.

"The girls you interviewed today?"

"Oh, them. What about them?"

"Did you like any of them?"

"There's one girl that I think would be good."

"Is she ugly?"

"Lily!"

"Is she a lesbian?"

"Lily!"

"Come on, Luke, give me something here."

I grabbed the bottle of wine from the nightstand and asked Lily to hand me her glass. As I poured some in, I began to tell her about Cody.

"Her name is Cody Chase and she's very qualified. She has plenty of secretarial experience and she's great with computers."

"What does she look like?" she asked.

"I don't know, Lily. To be honest, I didn't even notice."

"Liar."

I chuckled. "Babe, you're killing me here. There's no reason for you to be acting like this."

She turned away, got up from the bed, and went into the bathroom, shutting the door behind her. She looked upset, but I didn't understand what I said to make her feel that way. I lightly knocked on the door.

"Lily, babe, are you okay?"

"I'm fine. I just had to pee."

She was lying because she never closed the door when she peed. I turned the knob and opened the door to find her leaning up against the counter with tears streaming down her face.

"What's wrong?" I asked as I walked over to her and wrapped my arms around her.

"I'm sorry, Luke."

"Was it something I said?" I asked as I gently wiped the tears from her eyes.

She nodded.

"Babe, talk to me."

"You said there's no reason for me to be acting like this. I have a reason and the reason is what led me to Santa Monica in the first place."

I closed my eyes because I felt like a complete bastard. I completely disregarded her fears and what Hunter did to her. I held her face in my hands.

"Look at me. I love you, Lily Gilmore. You and only you. I don't know how to make that any clearer to you."

"I know you do. This is something I need to work out for myself. It has nothing to do with you, Luke. It's what Brynn and Hunter did to me. I need to get over it."

"Maybe you should call Dr. Blakely and talk to her about it. I don't want you being upset about this. I need to hire an assistant, babe. I have no choice because I'm drowning."

She buried her face into my neck and softly brushed her lips against my skin.

"I know and I'm sorry. I love you, Luke, and I promise not to say another word about it. I feel like such an idiot."

I lightly smiled as I kissed the side of her head. "You are not an idiot." I moved my hand up her shirt and began to rub her back. She moaned and tilted her head back. My lips lightly brushed against her skin as I leaned in closer to her, pressing my hard cock up against her. Her hands traveled down to the button on my jeans as she unbuttoned it and took the zipper down. I stared into her beautiful eyes as I lifted her shirt over her head and quickly undid her bra, releasing her breasts and taking each one in my mouth. She released my cock, which was throbbing for her, and stroked it up and down in her soft hand. I lifted up her skirt, took down her panties, and grabbed her hips, setting her up on the bathroom counter.

"I need you inside me now," she whispered as I kissed her lips.

My fingers softly rubbed her clit and then found their way inside her, feeling her excitement. She was more than ready.

"You're ready for me, babe," I said in between kisses as I brought her closer to the edge of the counter and pushed deep inside her with one thrust. We both gasped at the same time. She placed her hands on the counter and arched her back as I held on to her hips and moved in and out of her.

"Luke, oh my God."

"Come for me, babe. You're so wet and I want more. I want to feel you come all over me."

Her moans heightened and I felt her tighten around me. She was ready to explode and so was I.

"Lily, I can't hold back anymore."

She wrapped her arms around me and dug her nails into my back as we both came together. I slowly moved in and out of her as I poured every last drop of pleasure inside her. We smiled at each other as I pushed a few strands of her hair behind her ear.

"I'll never be able to get enough of you. We could make love a million times in our lives and it still wouldn't be enough," I said.

She brought her finger up to my mouth and traced the outline of my lips, then softly brushed hers against them. Her legs were still wrapped tightly around me and I was still inside of her. I picked her up from the counter and carried her into the bedroom, lying her down on the bed and hovering over her.

"Do you feel that?" I asked as I took her hard nipple in my mouth.

"Yes." She laughed.

"Shall we?"

"Of course." She smiled.

Chapter 7

Lily

I started the day off by making pancakes for Luke. I knew he had to get to the bar and I had to get to the studio, so I got up extra early and made sure they were ready when he woke up.

"It smells delicious in here, babe," he said as he poured some coffee.

"Thanks. The pancakes will be done in a second. Go sit down."

He walked up behind me and put his hands on my hips and nuzzled his face into my neck.

"I love it when you're bossy."

I heard my phone beep in the bedroom and I asked Luke if he could grab it for me while I put the pancakes on his plate.

"Who's Cameron?" he asked as he held up my phone.

"Oh. What did he say?"

"He said that he'll meet you at the studio at ten o'clock."

"Great. I'll trade you." I smiled as I held up his plate.

Luke handed me my phone and stood there, staring at me. "Are you going to tell me who the guy is that's texting you and meeting you at ten o'clock?"

"You're cute when you're jealous." I smiled. "He's the contractor that Giselle set me up with. He's coming to see what work needs to be done."

I sat down at the table with Luke and replied to Cameron's text message.

"Sounds great. I'll be there."

I couldn't believe this was finally happening. I was going to own my own photography studio. The first pictures I would hang on the wall would be of Rory and the girls. I also thought I could go through the pictures that I took on my road trip when I left Seattle. I hadn't looked at those pictures since I developed them in Portland almost two years ago.

"Hello. Babe." Luke waved.

I snapped out of my daze and looked at him.

"Are you okay?"

"Sorry. I was just in la-la land over my new studio. There's so much to do."

"Don't stress about it. I'll help you any way I can," he said.

"I know you will."

Luke finished his coffee and pancakes and got up from the table to finish getting dressed. As I cleaned up, Luke's phone beeped with a text message that flashed across the screen.

"Bro, are you hiring that hot babe today? If you are, I'll be hanging out at the bar more often."

I felt sick, but I couldn't let Luke know I read it. I needed to get my insecurities under control and maybe talking to Dr. Blakely wasn't such a bad idea.

"Okay, babe. I'm off," Luke said as he kissed me goodbye and grabbed his phone from the counter. "Have a great day at the studio and I'll see you later."

"Bye, baby. I love you."

"I love you too," he said as he walked out the door.

****

I stepped into the studio, turned on the lights, and took in a deep breath. The door opened and, when I turned around, there was a hot guy standing there.

"Hi, you must be Lily. I'm Cameron Cole." He smiled as he held out his hand.

"Hi, Cameron, it's nice to meet you. Thank you for meeting me here today."

"No problem. Thank you for getting in contact with me. So, this is going to be a photography studio?" he asked.

"Yes, and if you'll follow me, I'll explain my vision to you."

We talked for almost two hours and then he took measurements. I told him my ideas. He gave me some of his, which were great, and things I didn't think of, and then he told me he could start tomorrow.

"Thank you again, Cameron. I'll see you tomorrow."

"You're welcome, Lily. Enjoy the rest of your day." He smiled.

I had so much to do and many supplies to order. Cameron said it would only take about a week to do what he needed to get done, so I got online and ordered the equipment and supplies I needed for the studio. I looked at the clock and it was lunchtime. I decided to go by the bar and tell Luke that Cameron was going to start tomorrow. When I walked in, I saw Luke sitting at a table, eating lunch with a woman sitting across from him. I instantly felt sick.

"Hey, Lily." Maddie smiled.

"Hi, Maddie."

"Luke is right over there."

"Yeah, I saw him."

I walked over to the table, and as soon as Luke saw me, he stood up and gave me a kiss.

"Lily. What are you doing here, babe?"

"I thought maybe we could have lunch together, but I see you're already eating."

"Cody, I want you to meet my girlfriend, Lily. Lily, this is Cody, my new assistant."

She was pretty. Too pretty. The kind of pretty that would make any woman extremely jealous having her working so closely with their husbands or boyfriends. Her short, brown hair looked perfect on her and she had piercing green eyes.

"It's nice to meet you, Lily." She smiled as she held out her hand.

"It's nice to meet you too." I smiled with such a fakeness I thought my face was going to fall off. "I don't want to interrupt you. So I'm just going to get going."

"No, babe, stay. Have lunch with us," Luke pleaded.

"No. That's okay. You two have a lot to discuss. I should have called you first," I said as I walked towards the door.

I couldn't get out of there fast enough. It felt like my airways were constricted and I was unable to breathe. I pushed the door open and as soon as I stepped outside, Luke took hold of my arm.

"Are you okay?"

"I'm fine."

"Please, Lily, stay and have lunch with us."

"I don't want to. I'm sorry, but I have to go."

"It's because of Cody. Isn't it?"

I put my hand on his chest and stared into his eyes as I softly spoke. "Listen to me. You go finish your lunch and show Cody the ropes. That way, you'll be able to get back home to me quicker."

"Are you sure?" he asked.

"More than sure." I smiled.

He softly kissed my lips and then walked back inside. I pulled out my phone and dialed Dr. Blakely.

"Dr. Blakely's office. This is Camille. How can I help you?"

"Hi, Camille. It's Lily Gilmore. I need to see Dr. Blakely as soon as possible."

"Okay, Miss Gilmore, let me see what her schedule looks like. She has an opening at one o'clock."

"I'll take it and I'll see you then." *Click.*

I looked at my watch and saw it was twelve fifteen, so I decided to walk down the street to Starbucks. As I was standing in line, I heard someone call my name.

"Hey, Adam." I waved.

I took my sandwich and coffee over to his table and sat down. "Are you studying?" I asked.

"Yeah. For some weird reason, I study better in a Starbucks setting."

I laughed. "How are you? I haven't seen you in a while."

"I'm good. How are you?"

I shifted in my seat as I bit into my sandwich. "I'm okay." I smiled. "The contractor is going to start work on the studio tomorrow morning. So I can't complain."

He sat there and stared at me, knowing I wasn't telling him something.

"Anything else? I can tell something's bothering you."

"It must be your counselor instincts, right?"

He chuckled. "Yeah, I guess so."

"It's just me being stupid about something. Luke hired this beautiful girl to be his assistant and I'm having some issues with it. I just walked in on them having lunch at the bar and nearly had a panic attack and had to get out of there. I have an appointment with my therapist at one o'clock."

"It's understandable for you to have certain fears about that, considering what you've been through, but Luke is a great guy and I have a lot of respect for him. He would never cheat on you."

"I know he wouldn't. That's why I don't understand why I feel the way I do."

"You'll figure it out, Lily. Just take things one day at a time. You're going to be so busy with your new studio that you're not going to have time to give that girl a second thought."

"You're right." I smiled as I looked at my watch. "I better get going and you better get back to studying. Thanks for the talk."

"You're welcome, Lily."

I got up from my seat and walked back to the bar parking lot to get my car. As I approached, I saw Luke around the front, showing off his motorcycle to Cody. I already hated her. Knots began to form in my stomach. I turned down another street that led to the back of his parking lot because I didn't want him to see me. I hopped in the Explorer and drove to Dr. Blakely's office.

Chapter 8

Luke

I could already tell that Cody was going to be a life saver. She really seemed to know her stuff. Lily looked very uncomfortable when she walked over to the table and I thought she was pissed when she saw us eating together.

"How long have you been dating your girlfriend?" Cody asked.

"About seven months." I smiled.

"And how about you?" Lucky said as he strolled in.

Cody smiled and shook her head. "Let's just say that I'm in between boyfriends at the moment."

"Perfect. It just so happens that I'm in between girlfriends."

"Don't listen to him, Cody. He's living with a woman and she's having his baby."

She looked at him in disgust. "How dare you," she said.

"What? We have an open relationship. She sees other guys all the time. In fact, we're having some people over for dinner tonight. Why don't you join us and you can meet all of our friends."

"Are you going?" she asked me.

"Yeah."

"Okay. Thanks for the invite, Lucky. I look forward to it."

I sent Cody to the office to start on some paperwork and then I grabbed Lucky by the arm.

"What the fuck, dude? How could you invite her? Why would you invite her? I told you that Lily isn't comfortable with this situation."

"Relax, bro. Lily will be fine."

I rolled my eyes and went into my office. I didn't know if I should have told Lily that Cody was going to be there tonight or not. Fuck Lucky for putting me in this position. I went about my day and made sure I left the bar early enough to go home, shower, and change before the clusterfuck of the night was going to start.

****

When I walked through the door, Lily was sitting at the table on her laptop. I walked up behind her and softly kissed her neck.

"It's so good to be home."

She cupped the back of my neck with her hand and tilted her head to the side, so I had better access to her soft skin.

"It's good to have you home."

My hands cupped her breasts and squeezed them tightly. I wanted her and I wanted her now.

"Stand up, Lily," I said.

She did as I asked and I lifted her shirt over her head and unclasped her bra, throwing it onto the floor.

"Luke," she moaned as I took her breast in my mouth.

I unbuttoned her shorts and pulled them down, along with her panties, as my tongue slid down her torso and to her clit. Her moans became louder as I pleasured her with my mouth. She was swollen and about to come.

"Don't stop, Luke. I'm going to come!" she yelled.

I flicked my tongue around her clit before softly sucking it and plunging my fingers deep inside her. That was all I needed to do to send her over the edge with an orgasm. Her fingers tightened through my hair as she gasped and moaned with pleasure. I stood up and took off my pants as she lifted my shirt over my head. She wrapped her fingers around my cock and stroked me as I passionately kissed her. There was no more time to waste. I picked her up and she wrapped her legs around me. I put her up against the wall as I thrust inside of her, never breaking our kiss. I moved in and out of her rapidly until I was about to come. I couldn't hold back anymore. I wanted nothing more than to release myself inside her. Her moans excited me. I loved knowing that I made her feel so fucking good. One last deep thrust and we both came together. As I buried my face into her neck and tried to catch my breath, she told me how much she loved me.

"I love you, too, babe." I smiled as I looked at her. "Don't you ever forget it."

She released her legs and I carefully set her down. As we were in the bathroom getting ready to go to Giselle's, Lily told me she went and saw Dr. Blakely.

"How did it go?"

"It went well. She pointed out a lot of things to me that I really never thought of."

Do I or don't I tell her about Cody? Damn Lucky. "Lucky was in the bar today and he invited Cody to dinner at Giselle's tonight."

She stopped putting on her mascara and stared at me through the mirror. "What?"

"I tried to stop him, but you know Lucky; he doesn't care and he doesn't listen."

"Okay."

"Okay? You're not going to yell at me?"

"Nope. It's not your fault and she seems like a nice girl. Maybe it wouldn't be such a bad idea to get to know her better since she's going to be working with you every day."

"You're amazing." I smiled as I kissed the side of her head.

"Yeah. I know." She winked.

****

Lily

An uneasiness settled inside me. Dr. Blakely said that Luke wasn't Hunter and I needed to remind myself of that. She also told me that if I ever wanted to be at peace with what had happened, it would be a good idea to talk to Brynn and Hunter and get my feelings out. I wasn't so sure about that. I was afraid that I'd murder both of them if I saw them face to face. Brynn still sent me text messages every once in a while, asking for my forgiveness. I never replied back. I just hit the delete button. According to my mother, the two of them were still together and, as far as I was concerned, they deserved each other. Luke and I arrived at Giselle's house fifteen minutes late.

"It's about time," she said as she hugged me.

"Sorry. Luke kind of had me pinned to a wall."

"Oh my. I can't wait to get that kind of action on again. It's kind of hard right now with the large baby bump and all." She laughed as she rubbed her tummy.

Luke walked right over to where Sam was standing, talking to Cody. Gretchen walked up to me and hooked her arm around mine. Giselle did the same and they walked me outside on the patio.

"Who the fuck is that Cody chick and why is she here?" Gretchen asked.

"Luke's new assistant and compliments of a douchebag named Lucky," I said as I looked over at Giselle.

"He's an asshole. You already know that," she said.

"I saw Dr. Blakely today and she said a few things that helped. So, I'm trying not to think about how gorgeous Cody is and how she'll see my boyfriend more than I do every day." A tear started to form in my eye.

"What are the three of you doing out here?" Luke asked as he and Sam stepped out the door.

"Having girl talk. Would you care to join in on our birthing conversation?" Gretchen asked.

"Um. No. I think we're good. Right, Luke?"

"Yeah. We are totally good. Go back to talking and we'll see you inside."

The three of us laughed. "So, did you find out the sex of the baby?" I asked.

"The answer is in that big box in the living room. I brought in a bunch of blue and pink balloons to the doctor's office and I had the nurse find out the sex of the baby and then put the appropriate color balloons in the box. So, when we open the box, we'll all know at the same time."

"What a fabulous idea. I'm so excited. Let's find out now."

"After dinner. It's almost ready. In fact, we should get back inside."

I noticed that Luke and Cody were talking alone. I walked over to where they were standing and made sure she knew he was mine. I wrapped my arms around him and laid my head on his shoulder. I was staking my claim.

"Hey, babe. Are the three of you done with your conversation?"

"Yes, we are, and it's almost time to eat, so we better sit down."

I was on alert as to where Cody thought she was sitting. Next thing I knew, Lucky took hold of her arm and led her to the seat next to his. Luke and I sat down and he poured me a glass of wine. I smiled and thanked him with a kiss on the lips. Giselle kept looking at me and rolling her eyes as Lucky fed Cody his lines of bullshit. Once dinner was over, we all gathered into the living room and sat down, except for Giselle and Lucky, who stood in the center of the room behind the box.

"Okay. Is everyone ready to find out what gender our kid is?" Giselle asked with a smile.

Lucky carefully ran the box opener across the top and a bunch of pink balloons came out. Lucky hugged Giselle and everyone screeched and clapped, but I thought Luke was the loudest when he stood up and yelled, "YES! THANK YOU, GOD!"

Gretchen and I ran over to Giselle and hugged her tightly.

"Dude, what the hell was that for?" Lucky asked Luke.

"Paybacks. You're having a daughter and there will be guys exactly like you trying to get into her pants."

"The hell they will. My daughter isn't allowed to date and I will protect her against guys like me."

I looked at Lucky and smiled as I hugged him. "Congratulations on your baby girl. May you have many sleepless nights when she's a teenager."

"You two are mean people," Lucky pointed out.

Giselle was so excited that she was having a girl that she could barely stand it. Luke and I decided it was time for us to leave because he needed to be at the bar early in the morning and I had to be at the studio.

Chapter 9

Lily

Two weeks later…

The studio was finally finished and everything was set in its place. Cameron did an amazing job and I couldn't be happier. I hung up Rory's picture of her and the girls and a few of Charley that I'd taken. Giselle and Gretchen stopped by a lot and helped me organize things. In just a few short days, the doors would be ready to open.

Later that night, Luke got home from the bar later than usual. When he walked in, I could instantly tell he was in a bad mood.

"What's wrong?" I asked as he walked over and gave me a kiss.

"Just a bad day, babe. The liquor order didn't show up today, the dishwasher broke, and the toilet overflowed."

"I'm sorry."

He walked to the refrigerator and grabbed a beer. He threw the cap on the counter and looked at the box that was sitting on the table.

"What's in the box?"

"Pictures I took when I left Seattle. I just took it down from the closet shelf. I haven't opened it or looked in it since I first arrived in Portland and had them developed. I was going to see if there were any pictures I could blow up and put in the studio."

"Great idea, babe. Do you mind if I open it?"

"No. Go right ahead. I have to brush my teeth real quick. I'll be back in a second."

I went into the bathroom and brushed my teeth. When I walked back into the living room, the pictures from the box were scattered all over the table and floor and Luke stood there and did nothing but stare at me. I stopped dead in my tracks because suddenly I got the feeling that something was wrong.

"Luke, what is it?"

The look on his face was one of pure anger. It was a look that I'd never seen before.

"Luke! What's going on?"

"It was you," he said with a low voice.

"It was me what? What are you talking about?"

He held out a picture to me. I walked over and took it from him and gasped when I saw the couple sitting at the table. It was Luke and Callie. Tears immediately filled my eyes as I looked at him.

"You were the woman who gave us the tickets to Aruba. It was you. The night Callie was killed was the night that we were on our way home from the airport from Aruba. The trip YOU gave to us."

I began to shake and I felt like I was going to pass out. "Luke. I—"

"You what, Lily? Answer me one question. "Did you remember me when you saw me?"

"NO! Of course not. I would have said something. You didn't remember me?"

"I thought you sort of looked familiar, but I blew it off when I found out that you were Johnny's daughter. I can't believe this. I can't believe that I—"

"That you what? What exactly are you saying?" I yelled as tears poured down my face.

"If you had never given us those tickets, we wouldn't have gone, and Callie would still be alive today."

The knife that plunged into my heart at that moment hurt like nothing else. I'd never felt such pain as I did right then. Not even when I caught Brynn and Hunter together. This pain was far worse and something I'd never experienced before.

"Are you blaming me for Callie's death?" I screamed.

He stood there and then turned away. "I guess I am. I have to get out of here," he said as he walked to the bedroom and slammed the door shut.

I felt so shaky and out of it that I needed to sit down on the couch before I collapsed. I couldn't believe what had just happened and I couldn't believe Luke blamed me for Callie's death. He came out of the bedroom with his bag and headed towards the door.

"Where are you going?" I cried as I jumped up from the couch and grabbed his hand.

He jerked away from me. "I can't stay here for a while. I need to think about things."

"Think about what? Please don't leave me, Luke."

"I need space, Lily. This is too much for me to handle right now."

"If you walk out that door, then you're blaming me for Callie's death and that's not fair."

"I'm leaving before we both say something we'll regret."

"It's too late! You already said it!" I screamed as he walked out the door.

I grabbed my head and paced back and forth. I picked up the box from the table and threw it against the door. I fell to my knees and sobbed like a baby. How could he do this to me? How could he blame me and then walk out and ruin us? I didn't know what to do. I needed him. I needed him to hold me and tell me that everything was going to be all right. I curled up into a ball in the middle of the floor and didn't move.

Chapter 10

Luke

"What the fuck is going on?" Sam yelled as I slammed the door shut.

"Leave me alone," I said as I stormed into the bedroom.

He followed me. "Gretchen and I could hear you and Lily screaming next door. What happened, man?"

I looked at Sam, who was standing in the doorway, and Gretchen was behind him.

"You want to know what the fuck happened? I'll tell you. Lily had a box of pictures she took when she left Seattle. There was a picture of me and Callie. She was the girl who gave us the tickets to Aruba!"

"So what? What the fuck are you saying, Luke?"

"If she never would have given me and Callie those tickets, the accident never would have happened."

Sam closed his eyes and shook his head. "Oh my God, Luke. Please tell me you didn't say that to Lily."

Suddenly, Gretchen went flying out the door and I assumed over to Lily's apartment.

"Get out, Sam. I don't want to be bothered. I need to think and I can't do it with you and Gretchen here. Can the two of you go stay somewhere else?"

"Really, Luke? You can't stay with Lily, but it's okay to stay next door? Fuck you. Gretchen and I aren't going anywhere. You need to grow the fuck up, man. How dare you blame Lily? In fact, I hope she never speaks to you again."

I grabbed my bag. "Fuck this. I'll leave."

I strapped the bag to my bike and took off to my parents' house. They had just left for another cruise and wouldn't be back for two weeks. My mind was a total clusterfuck. I didn't know what to think or what to do. I just needed to get really drunk and forget about it, at least for tonight.

****

Lily

I heard the door open and, for a second, I thought it was Luke coming back to tell me he was sorry, until I heard Gretchen's voice.

"Lily," she whispered as she walked over to me, got down on the floor, and wrapped her arms around me.

"I don't know what happened. One second, we were so happy and the next, he's leaving. I had no idea that he was the one I gave the tickets to. I never opened that box after I developed the pictures."

"I know, sweetie. Come on; get up and at least lie down on the couch."

She helped me up and over to the couch. I sat there as the tears poured down my face and Gretchen tried to console me. There was nothing anyone could say or do at this point to make me feel better.

"I need a drink," I cried.

"I'll get you a beer."

"No. There's a bottle of wine in the rack."

Gretchen got up and grabbed the wine with two glasses and sat down. The door opened and Sam walked in.

"Lily. I'm so sorry," he said as he walked over and put his arm around me.

I buried my face into his chest and cried some more.

"Just give him some time, Lily. He's just freaked out right now. He'll come around."

"What if he doesn't? What if he hates me forever? He blamed me, Sam. He pretty much said that I killed Callie. How the fuck am I supposed to go on? He's my life. Finding Hunter and Brynn on my wedding day was nothing compared to this."

"You won't have to. He'll come around. He's Luke, and even though he's a fuckhead right now, we all know what an amazing person he is."

"I need to be alone right now," I said as I looked at Sam and Gretchen.

"Okay. We're right next door if you need us."

As soon as they left, I grabbed the bottle of wine and took it to the bedroom. I wasted no time downing half of it before I lay down and pretty much passed out.

Chapter 11

Luke

When I arrived at my parents' house, I threw my bag down in the hallway and headed to the bar area in the living room. I took out the whiskey bottle, grabbed a glass, and went outside to the patio. It wasn't too long before I polished off half the bottle. I was so angry. Angry that Lily and I had met before and neither one of us remembered. Angry that she was the one to give us the tickets to Aruba. Angry that the accident happened on the way home from the airport. Angry that I had to find out. There was no reasoning with me at this point. Once the shock settled, I would be able to process things better. But for now, I was ready to pass out.

I awoke the next morning to the constant ringing of my phone. I rolled over and grabbed it from the other side of the bed to see that Maddie was calling.

"Hello," I sleepily answered.

"Luke, where are you? Aren't you coming in today? I've been trying to call you and Lily all morning and there's been no answer. What the hell is going on?"

"I'll be there soon." *Click.*

I sighed as I rubbed my face and jumped in the shower. As I let the hot water run down me, I felt numb. When I finished,

I got dressed, grabbed my keys, hopped on my bike, and drove to the bar.

"You look like shit," Maddie said as I walked in. "Cody has been waiting for you. What the hell is going on?"

"I don't want to talk about it right now," I said as I walked past her.

I went in my office and Cody was sitting behind my desk.

"Good morning, boss. Or should I say 'afternoon.'" She smiled.

"Sorry. I had a rough night."

"Are you okay?"

"Yeah. Record all the receipts from last night. That should be the first thing you do when you come in."

"Already done."

"Oh. Well, then get my files organized. I'll have a desk moved in here so you don't have to sit at mine."

I walked out and went behind the bar. I grabbed a bottle of beer and opened it. Maddie was standing there, staring at me and giving me a disgusted look.

"I found out last night that Lily was the woman who gave me the tickets to Aruba."

"How did you find that out?" she asked.

"I found a picture she took of Callie and me in Portland. It was in a box with a bunch of other pictures she took when she left Seattle."

"Okay. So then what?"

"We argued. We fought. I screamed. If she never would have given us those tickets, Callie would still be alive today."

Maddie's eyes widened. "Luke, no. Are you blaming Lily for the accident?"

I brought the bottle up to my lips and took a long swig of it before answering her.

"Maybe I am. Maddie, you have to understand where I'm coming from," I pleaded. If anyone would get me, it would be my sister. "If we didn't go to Aruba, we wouldn't have been on our way home that night from the airport and that accident never would have happened and Callie would still be alive."

Her eyes filled with tears as she stared at me. "Luke, Lily means the world to you. The two of you are so in love. You can't possibly forget that. Did you tell her that you blamed her?"

I nodded.

"Oh my God, Luke. I can't even imagine someone saying that to me. I love you, but you're wrong."

"Somehow, I knew you'd take her side."

"It's not about sides. What are you going to do?"

"I have no clue. I just need some time away to think. I can't do that here surrounded by everyone. Will you be okay to run the bar while I'm gone?"

"Yeah, but where are you going?"

"I'm going to rent a cabin for a couple of days in the mountains and go hiking. It's the best way to think."

"Please be careful," she said as she kissed my cheek.

I gave her a small smile and left the bar. I contacted Joe, a friend of my parents who owned a string of cabins in the mountains. He had one cabin left and I reserved it. I headed back to my parents' house and then over to my apartment to get my hiking boots and jeep. As soon as I walked through the door, I saw Gretchen standing in the kitchen. She turned and looked at me and then turned back around without saying a word.

"I know you're pissed off at me and I'm sorry."

"I'm not the one you should be apologizing to," she snapped.

"I'm going away for a couple of days."

"I don't really care," she snapped again.

"Have you talked to Lily?" I asked with hesitation.

She turned around with anger in her eyes and pointed her spoon at me. "That, mister, is none of your fucking business. If you care so much, then go and talk to her and find out how she is yourself," she yelled as she stomped away and into the bedroom.

I grabbed my boots and stepped into the hallway, locking the door behind me while I stared at Lily's door. Fuck. I shook my head and headed to the jeep.

****

Lily

I tried to open my eyes, but they were too puffy and swollen shut. I had nightmares last night. Nightmares about the accident. I needed to talk to Luke. I picked up my phone and, through my swollen eyes, I sent him a text message.

"Please come over and talk to me. I'm begging you, Luke."

I waited a few minutes and there was no response.

"Please, Luke. We can talk this out. We can work through this."

Still, no response. I didn't have the strength to do anything. All I wanted to do was sleep. Suddenly, there was a knock on the door and I heard Giselle's voice.

"Lily, are you in there? Open the door before I break it down."

I stumbled out of bed and out of the bedroom to unlock the door. As soon as I opened it, Giselle threw her arms around me.

"I'm so sorry. Gretchen called last night, but she said you kicked her and Sam out and didn't want to be bothered."

"I can't do this, Giselle." I began to cry.

Her hands firmly clasped my shoulders. "Yes, you can! This is a bump in the road where your relationship is concerned. As soon as that bump is smoothed out, everything will be fine and go back to normal."

"Not this time. You didn't see the anger on his face. You didn't see the hate in his eyes. You didn't hear the disgust in his voice."

"He'll realize he's being an ass and come begging for your forgiveness," she said.

"I'm such a mess and I can't even believe this happened," I continued to sob.

"Shh, sweetie. Do you want me to talk to him? Because I'll punch him in the balls for you. I've done it before and I'll do it again." She smiled.

I let out a light laugh in between sobs. Giselle was the one who always had a way of making light of a horrible situation.

"Go shower and I'll make you some coffee. You're a hot mess right now and you'll feel better after a hot shower."

I nodded and slowly walked to the bathroom. Once I was in the shower and the hot water was beating down my back, the tears started up again and I crouched down in the corner and sobbed.

Chapter 12

Luke

On the way up to the cabin, I received Lily's text messages. I couldn't bring myself to answer her back. I needed time to sort things out; my feelings and my anger. I finally arrived to the cabin where Joe was waiting for me with the keys.

"Well, if it isn't Luke Matthews. Long time no see, buddy." He smiled as we lightly hugged.

"Pastor Joe, how are you?"

"I'm good. How are you doing?"

"I'm okay."

"What brings you up here?"

"I have a lot on my mind and a lot of thinking to do."

"Your mom and dad told me you finally bought Bernie's Bar."

"Yeah, I did."

"Well, here's your keys. The place has everything you need. It's the same one you used to stay in with your parents as a kid."

"I can see that. Thank you."

"If you need anything, I'll just be down the road."

"Thanks, Joe."

I walked through the door and looked around. Nothing had changed. I set my bags down and walked out to the back where the lake was. I'd been wanting to bring Lily here for quite a while, but with the bar, I hadn't had the time. I knew she'd like it here. It was peaceful and quiet and it would have been just the two of us, like she was always asking. My phone beeped in my pocket, and when I pulled it out, I had a text message from Lucky.

"Dude, you're fucking crazy. How could you do that to Lily of all people? You need to talk to her. I know I'm no authority on relationships, but I look up to yours."

"You don't understand, so drop it. I want everyone to leave me alone for a while. Tell Sam that I've gone up to the cabin."

"You're crazy, bro. I hate to say this, but I'm really disappointed in you."

I didn't respond. He didn't understand. Nobody understood. I wasn't sure if I even understood. I hopped in my jeep and drove to the liquor store for a case of beer and a pizza.

****

Lily

For the first time in seven months, I was alone. Alone in my apartment like I was when I first arrived here. Being alone was fine before I met Luke. But then he came into my life, swept me off my feet, and loved me like no other person ever had.

And now he was gone. I walked to the living room where Giselle had picked up all the pictures and put them back in the box. I didn't want to see that box ever again. I picked it up off the counter and as I opened the door to go and throw it in the dumpster, Maddie was standing there.

"Hey, Lily. I didn't know if you were home. I'm not even going to ask you how you're doing because I already know."

"Come on in, Maddie."

I couldn't turn her away and now I was worried about Charley and how she would react to the news of Luke and me not being together anymore.

"Have you eaten, Lily?" she asked.

I shook my head. Food was the last thing on my mind. The truth was that if I even attempted to put food in my mouth, I'd probably throw it up.

"You need to eat. Let's go out somewhere. I know you probably don't want to, but it'll be good for you to get out, even if it's only for a couple of hours."

"I can't, Maddie."

"Yes, you can. Go grab your purse and let's go. We'll go somewhere small where there's not a lot of people."

She was persistent and I knew she was trying to help. Maybe getting out of this apartment for a couple of hours was what I needed.

We hopped into her car and she drove us to a cute little diner. When we walked in, we were instantly seated.

"Luke will come around," she said as she grabbed my hand. "He's just upset right now but once he calms down, he'll be back."

"He never should have left. He should have stayed and talked to me. I know we could have worked this out. I swear to you, Maddie, that I had no idea he was the one I gave the tickets to. I swear."

"Sweetie, stop. I believe you, and Luke will too."

"Luke doesn't care about that. He only cares that I gave him the tickets, which in turn led to the accident that killed Callie."

"He's an ass and I don't want you to listen to him."

"I sent him a couple of text messages earlier and he never responded."

"He might not have gotten them. He's up at a cabin in the mountains and the service is not all that great."

"Why did he go there?"

"He said he needed to think and clear his head."

I sat there in disbelief that Luke would just leave town like that. I knew he was pissed and upset, but I never thought he would leave town.

"Once he has time to think things over, he'll be back and at your door."

Something inside me started to happen. Something that I'd never expected. I was becoming angry. Angry that he said what he did and angry that he blamed me for Callie's death. I was going back to that place I was at almost two years ago. The place where anger was comforting and consumed my life.

"Well, I may not be around if he does decide he was wrong."

Maddie looked at me and smiled. "You have every right to be upset with him."

She didn't even know the half of it. I ordered a bowl of chicken noodle soup and Maddie ordered a sandwich. I could barely eat and, with every bite I took, I wanted to vomit.

Chapter 13

Luke

I spent a few extra days than I originally anticipated at the cabin. Maddie said everything was fine with the bar and to take as much time as I needed. Pastor Joe stopped by one evening and brought a large pizza with him. He said we had some catching up to do before I went back home. We took the pizza out on the patio and I talked to him all about Lily.

"Listen, Luke. We're all on a timeline. We never know when the big guy upstairs plans to take us back home. As much as I hate to say it, it was Callie's time to go home and that accident would have happened anyway. Maybe you would have gone out to dinner that night. You don't know and you never will, but blaming Lily for Callie's death was not the right thing to do. You've let your anger for that accident cloud your judgment."

"I know I have," I said as I took a sip of my beer.

"There's a plan for all of us. People just don't come into our lives by accident. They come with a purpose. You were at the lowest point of your life after Callie died and then when you least expected it, Lily walked into your life. Do you think it's a coincidence? Do you believe in fate? When one door closes, no matter how painful it is, another opens for a greater purpose."

I sighed as I sat there and listened to him. "I get what you're saying, Joe. I really do. I think I just needed these last few days to clear my head and get over the shock. I mean, how the heck is it possible that Lily was the one to give us those tickets and then, a year later, show up in Santa Monica and move in next door?"

"That was the higher power doing his job, my son. Have faith and believe." He smiled as he patted my shoulder. "I best be going now. I have to prepare for a funeral tomorrow."

I got up from my seat and gave him a hug. "It was good seeing you, Joe. Thanks for the talk and for listening."

"No problem, Luke. It was good to see you again. Tell your parents that I expect to see them up here sometime soon. They keep going on those fancy cruises and I'm feeling a little unloved."

I chuckled. "I will."

I brought the plates and beer bottles into the kitchen and grabbed my phone. I missed Lily and I wanted to get home to her. God, I had a lifetime of making up to do to her and I owed her a huge explanation. I loved her so much and I wanted to spend the rest of my life with her. I decided to send her a text message.

"Hi, Lily. I'll be coming back to Santa Monica tomorrow and we need to talk."

I waited for a response. Nothing. I set my phone down and jumped into the shower. When I was finished, I looked at my phone again and still no response. Shit.

****

Lily

I spent the last few days locked in my apartment. The only time I left was when I went to dinner with Maddie. Gretchen, Giselle, and Sam kept calling and checking up on me and even Lucky stopped by for a visit. I hopped into my Explorer and drove to my appointment with Dr. Blakely.

"Come in, Lily. I'm glad you're here. You really had me worried on the phone."

"Thanks, Dr. Blakely," I said as I took a seat in the oversized leather chair.

"Have you heard from Luke?" she asked.

"No. I sent him a couple of text messages, but he never responded."

"I want you to tell me how you're feeling right now."

"I'm sad and hurt, but most of all, I'm angry. I'm really angry!" I spewed.

"That's understandable. Words can hurt louder than actions. I think you and Luke both have issues you need to work on. His issue is with Callie's death. I don't think he ever put closure on that and then there's your issues with your sister and Hunter."

I sat there, playing with a piece of string that was hanging from the bottom of my shirt.

"He pretty much called me a murderer. He blames me for Callie's death and maybe he's right. Why did I have to give those tickets away? I should have just thrown them in the garbage. I don't know if he'll ever forgive me."

"Saying never is pretty harsh."

"Yeah, well my life has been pretty harsh."

"What if he were to walk through that door right now and beg for your forgiveness. What would you do?"

"I don't know because, right now, I'm so angry."

"Angry at what? Him or the fact you gave him the tickets?"

"Both."

"Are you still angry at Brynn and Hunter?"

"Yes."

"Your mother?"

"We're working on our relationship. Things are going well with her right now."

"Good. Then you need to resolve your anger one step at a time. You can't go through life being angry. You will never be your true self and it'll always get in the way of your life."

"Maybe you should be telling Luke that," I said.

Her phone chimed, alerting us that my session was over. I got up from my seat, thanked her, and walked out of her office. I climbed in my Explorer and put my head down on the steering wheel. I was being forced to go back to the place I swore I'd never go back to.

****

Luke

Lily not responding to my message told me that she didn't want to talk to me. I dialed her number and it went straight to voicemail. I dialed Sam.

"Hey, Luke. How are you?" he answered.

"Hey, is Lily home?"

"I don't know, bro. Gretchen and I are out to dinner. Why?"

"I texted her earlier and she never texted me back."

"Do you fucking blame her? I wouldn't text you back either."

"Thanks, bro. I'll be home tomorrow. If you see Lily, tell her that I need to talk to her."

"I will, man. Safe travels."

I sighed as I hung up the phone. I opened another bottle of beer, lay down on the bed, and scrolled through the pictures of me and Lily on my phone. I slowly ran my finger across Lily's face, taking in how happy she looked, and how I had possibly destroyed her world. I had been in shock over my discovery. I said things I didn't mean. Words that I would take back in a heartbeat. She had to forgive me, because if she didn't, I didn't know what I'd do. I wanted to call her and just hear her voice, but I was scared. If she didn't respond to my text message, she wouldn't pick up the phone either. I needed to stop thinking and go to sleep for the night. Tomorrow would be a new day and beginning for me and Lily. I was going to make sure of it and get down on my hands and knees and beg her for forgiveness.

Chapter 14

Lily

I booked a non-stop flight to Seattle. I packed my suitcase and, when I walked out the door, Sam was coming out of his apartment. He looked at me and then at my suitcase.

"Hey, Lily. Where are you going?"

"I'm flying to Seattle for a while. I have some things I need to take care of there."

"Ah. I see. I talked to Luke last night. He said he sent you a text message, but you never responded."

"I didn't get a text message from him," I said as I pulled out my phone and took a second look.

"He's at the cabin and service isn't the best up there. Anyway, he's coming home today and he wanted me to tell you that he needs to talk to you."

"Well, that's too bad because I'm leaving. He had a chance to talk to me the day he left me sobbing hysterically in the middle of my apartment. Now he thinks that he's had time and that it's okay just to come back and want to talk? It doesn't work that way, Sam. I'm hurt, distraught, and to be honest, I feel betrayed. He doesn't just get to talk to me when it suits him. Now, if you'll excuse me, I have a plane to catch, and do me a favor, don't tell him where I am. Please."

The sadness in his eyes bothered me. But I had no choice.

"I won't tell him. Have a safe trip, Lily, and I'll see you when you get back," he said as he leaned over, kissed my cheek, and helped me load my suitcase in the back of the Explorer.

****

As I sat on the plane and stared out the window, I couldn't stop thinking about what Sam had said. Maybe Luke wanted to talk to me to put closure on our relationship because he still blamed me for what happened. The only thing I knew at this point was that my stomach was in a permanent knot and I'd never felt so lonely in my life. The plane landed and I rented a car and drove to my mom's house. The hardest part was going to be to have to face Brynn and possibly Hunter. I didn't care anymore what he did because I now realized that he wasn't my true love. But my sister, my baby sister, Brynn, was a different story. Blood doesn't do that to each other and it was mostly my anger with her that I needed to control.

****

Luke

I pulled up to the apartment building and Lily's Explorer wasn't there. Instead of going to my and Sam's apartment, I inserted the key into Lily's lock and opened the door. I looked around. Lily had all the blinds shut. There was a blanket lying on the couch and an empty bottle of wine sitting on the coffee table. I walked straight to the bedroom and she wasn't there. I opened the closet doors and noticed that some of her clothes were missing and her suitcase was gone. FUCK! Where the hell did she go? I pulled out my phone and texted Sam.

"Where's Lily?"

"I take it you're back. I don't know, dude. She said she was leaving and wouldn't tell me where she was going."

"What about her studio?"

"Don't know. She'll be back eventually. She didn't move for good."

"How the fuck do you know that?"

"She only had one suitcase. Chill out, Luke. You left and now so did she. Give her the space she wants."

I threw my bag down on the floor and headed to the bar. When I walked in, I saw Cody talking to Maddie.

"Well, look who's back." Maddie smiled.

"Do you know where Lily went?"

"No. I didn't know she left."

"Her suitcase is gone and so are some of her clothes. Sam said she wouldn't tell him where she was going."

"I'm not surprised, Luke. She was really broken up."

I shook my head and went to my office. A few moments later, Cody walked in.

"Hey, Luke. Welcome back and I'm really sorry. If there's anything I can do, just let me know."

"Thanks, Cody. Can you please shut the door on your way out?"

She nodded and walked out of the office. Sam was right. Lily didn't take all of her things, so she'd be back. I would have to wait until she was to talk to her and apologize.

****

Lily

I pulled up the driveway and an even worse sickness took over me. I walked up the steps of the porch and opened the front door with my shaking hand. I heard my mother's voice in the kitchen and, when I stood in the doorway, she turned and looked at me.

"Lily. What—"

The minute she said my name, the tears began to stream down my face.

"Oh, baby. Come here," she said as she held out her arms.

I walked over to her as she wrapped her arms around me and I cried, just like I did when I was a child.

"What happened?" she asked sympathetically as she walked me into the living room.

We sat down on the loveseat and I told her everything. Right down to the day I left Seattle.

"Lily, the accident was not your fault. How could he blame you like that?"

I told her exactly how I felt and the reason I came back here.

"Where's Brynn?" I asked as I wiped my eyes.

"She and Hunter went out. They'll be back later."

"So they're still together?" I asked. It was a subject that both of us avoided when we talked over the phone.

"Yes."

I asked my mother for a glass of wine, and when she went to get it, I sat there and thought about Hunter and Brynn. After all that happened, they were still together. Maybe that was why I was a part of Hunter's life. So he could meet Brynn. The two of them must have really loved each other to still be together. Maybe they had the passion that Luke and I did. I didn't know and I didn't want to know. I was handed my glass of wine and my mother asked me if she could get me something to eat. Food wasn't really on my agenda. I still became sick with each bite. I got up from the couch and took my suitcase up to my old room. It looked the same as it did the day I left.

"I never touched it," my mother said as she stood in the doorway. "The maids dust it once a week. I wanted it exactly the same in case you came back."

I looked out my window at the gazebo that sat in the middle of lawn, surrounded by flowers. My dad had it built for me when I was a kid. He told me that it was my very own special place to go when I was having a bad day or just needed to think. I liked to play my guitar there. Everyone, including the staff, knew that when I was in my gazebo, I wasn't to be disturbed. It was my sanctuary and my safe haven. A place where all my troubles disappeared the minute I stepped inside.

"Excuse me, Mother," I said as I walked out of my room and out to the gazebo.

I took in a deep breath before stepping inside because I wanted all my troubles to magically go away. After a few moments, I heard something. I froze in place and it seemed like time stood still.

"Hi, Lily," Brynn said with a soft voice.

I had to compose myself before turning around to face her. Once I took in several deep breaths, I slowly turned around and saw my sister standing there before me, with tears in her eyes.

"Brynn."

"It's so good to see you," she said nervously.

"We have a lot of talking to do," I said.

"I know. It's been a long time," she replied.

Looking at her didn't make me as sick to my stomach as I thought it would. Maybe it was because I was already sick enough over Luke. I looked across the way and saw our mother walking towards us.

"I think the two of you should go out to dinner. Talk over some greasy food like you used to. I think that maybe a public place would be best for your first time talk."

"I agree. Is Cabala's still around?" I asked Brynn.

"Yeah. It is. I'll drive." She smiled.

I climbed into her car and we drove off to the place that made the best lobster macaroni and cheese in the world. I could tell Brynn was uncomfortable and that she was on pins and needles waiting for me to explode and go off on her. But I didn't. I kept reminding myself of what Dr. Blakely said about letting anger consume me.

"Why, Brynn?" I finally asked.

"Do you want the truth?"

"Of course. That's all I ever wanted," I said.

She pulled into the parking lot of Cabala's and waited to spill the truth until we were seated.

"I fell in love with him and I don't know how it happened," she said as she looked down.

"Go on."

"I didn't want to hurt you and neither did he, but the attraction between us was stronger than we were and we didn't know how to stop it."

I set my menu down and looked at her. "You're my sister. How could you carry on with him the way you were and still have the nerve to look at me every day?"

"It was hard and unbearable. You have to believe me when I tell you that. I swear, Lily, neither one of us wanted it to happen, but it did."

I understood what Brynn was saying because it sounded like the same attraction that Luke and I had. When two people are meant to be together, there's nothing anyone can do to stop it.

"Do you know how many times I wanted to tell you? I tried on so many occasions, but I just couldn't."

"So instead, you were going to let me marry him? What were the two of you going to do, continue to fuck behind my back until I found out?"

"I don't know, Lily." She began to cry. "All I know is that I love him and I can't help how I feel. I'm so sorry for everything and I'm sorry for what I've done."

"But you and Hunter are still together. So how sorry could you be?"

She looked me straight in the eyes this time and, with a serious tone, she told me that they were in love. And there it was. They weren't just carrying on like two people who got off on the fact they knew it was wrong; they were supposed to be together and I was the middleman that helped make that happen. Could I be so reasonable? Would I forgive her? Would I forgive Hunter? I didn't know. I guessed that was something only time would tell.

Chapter 15

Luke

I left the bar and went for a ride on my motorcycle. I rode along the coast just like I used to do after Callie died. When I got back to the apartment, I unlocked my door. Gretchen and Sam were sitting at the table.

"Hey, bro," Sam said as he gave a small wave.

"Gretchen, do you know where Lily went?"

"No, and even if I did, I wouldn't tell you," she snapped.

I grabbed a beer from the fridge and sat down at the table next to them. Gretchen went to get up, and I grabbed her hand and asked her to sit down.

"Listen, I know you hate me right now, but I need to talk to Lily. I need to apologize to her for everything I've said and done. I can't lose her."

"Oh, so now you want to apologize? She trusted you. She gave herself to you when she swore off everything to do with love and relationships. She loved you so much that nothing else in this world mattered to her. And now you decide to come back, when it's convenient for you and try to fix things?"

"I know, Gretchen. I'm sorry. I will spend the rest of my life making it up to her. Please, do you know where she's at?"

"No, actually, I don't, but she'll be back when she's ready."

"Have you been in contact with her?" I asked.

"No. I haven't. She gave strict instructions to both Giselle and me not to call her or text her and that she'd talk to us when she's back. I'm sure she's fine. She's a strong woman."

Suddenly, there was a pounding at the door. Sam jumped up, and as soon as he opened the door, Charley came running in and over to me with tears in her eyes.

"Where's Lily, Uncle Luke?"

"Peanut, what are you doing here?"

"I'm sorry, Luke. She ran out of the apartment before I could stop her," Maddie said.

"Where is she?" Charley cried.

"I don't know, peanut. I'm trying to figure it out."

"I overheard my mom talking to my dad about how you blamed Lily for Callie's death."

I looked over at Maddie and gave her a stern look.

"I'm sorry. I thought she was asleep."

"She didn't cause Callie to die." She continued to cry.

"I know she didn't, peanut. I'm so sorry," I said as I grabbed her and hugged her.

She pushed me away. "I hate you for making Lily go away. I hate you!" she screamed as she ran out of the apartment.

Tears rolled down my face as I looked at Maddie and screamed Charley's name. Maddie left the apartment and I threw my bottle cap against the wall. "FUCK!" I screamed.

Sam walked over to me and put his hand on my shoulder. "I'm sorry, Luke. Just give it time. She'll be back and the two of you will work things out. You're meant to be together and you'll find a way."

"I hope so, Sam. I really do."

****

Lily

I was up in my room when I heard the front door open. My mom and I had plans to go shopping, but first, she had to run an errand, so we'd go when she came back. I grabbed my purse and stopped in the middle of the stairs when I saw Hunter standing in the foyer.

"Lily," he said.

"Brynn isn't home," I said as I continued down the stairs and into the kitchen.

"I know. I'm waiting for her. She told me that you and your mom were out shopping."

"She told you wrong," I said as I grabbed a bottle of water from the fridge.

"I think we need to talk."

"You think?" I snapped.

"I'm sorry, Lily. I really am. I know you hate me and you probably dream every day of new ways to murder me, and I don't blame you. I would too. But I am truly sorry. Your mom told me you found someone really great and I'm really happy for you."

I stood there and listened to his bullshit, taking in the stench behind every last word.

"Are you done?" I asked.

He looked nervous as he put his hands in his pockets and slowly nodded.

"Cancel your plans with Brynn; you're taking me to the park."

"What? I can't do that."

"You can and you will. I need to put this to rest and behind me once and for all."

He pulled out his phone, called Brynn, and told her what I had demanded. I called my mother and told her there was a change of plans and that I wouldn't be going shopping with her. She wanted to know what was going on and I told her that I'd explain later.

Hunter and I hopped into his BMW and headed to the park. It was the one place he always kept his promise and took me to.

"Why are you doing this, Lily?" he asked. "Why the park?"

"Why not? You said we needed to talk, so that's where we're going to do it."

"You're not secretly planning to kill me, are you?" he asked with seriousness.

"I can't make any promises."

He looked at me, and I busted out laughing. Oh my God, it was good to laugh again. As much as I hated him, he still could amuse me. As soon as we arrived at the park, we took a seat under a tree, just like we always did.

"After talking with Brynn, I can see that the two of you are really and seriously in love. I just wish you would have told me before we got so into the wedding. I don't get it, Hunter. Why? Why didn't you just tell me?"

"Because I didn't want to hurt you. Lily, I loved you. I really did, and every time Brynn and I would say it was over, we just couldn't seem to end it. I'm so sorry. You have no idea how many times I wanted to call you, but I couldn't because I truly hated myself for what I did to you. I guess you could say I was a coward."

I could hear the sincerity and remorse in his voice, just like I had heard it in Brynn's. The scar that the two of them left me would forever be there, but maybe with a little more understanding.

"Yes, you and Brynn were both cowards, but the fact that the two of you are still together tells me that you were meant to be with her and not me."

He reached over and lightly placed his hand on mine and I instantly jerked it away. "This doesn't mean we're going to be besties or anything like that."

"I know. Just the fact that you understand means the world to us. Why don't we all have dinner tonight?" he said.

"Don't push it."

I got up from the ground, wiped the dirt off my ass, and told him to take me home.

****

Luke

I went to the bar to check on things and, as soon as Candi saw me, she motioned for me to talk to her. I walked over behind the bar and grabbed the bottle of vodka and a glass.

"What's up, Candi?"

"I don't like that Cody girl you hired," she said.

"Why?"

"She's been nosing around, asking a bunch of questions about you and Lily. I think she likes you."

"There's no need to worry about her," I said as I downed my shot.

"I know her type, Luke, and she's looking to get you into bed."

"Like I said, don't worry about her. She's a good employee so far and if she crosses the line, I'll take care of it."

"Have you heard from Lily yet?" she asked.

"No. I guess I will when she's ready."

"I'm sorry, boss," she said as she put her hand on my shoulder.

"Yeah, me too." I walked away and headed straight to my office.

It was two a.m. and the last customer finally stumbled out. I helped the crew clean up and then walked the girls to their cars. When I got home, I headed straight for bed. I was tired and thinking about Lily all day wore me out, not to mention the fact that I was lonely as hell without her.

Chapter 16

Lily

I spent the last two weeks thinking about my life, thinking about the anger I had finally let go about Brynn and Hunter, but the anger I still harbored with Luke and his accusation that I was the one responsible for Callie's death. It had been over three weeks since I'd seen or talked to him, or anyone else, for that matter. My relationship with Brynn over the past couple of weeks was tolerable, but things would never be the same again. I thought about my studio and how I never opened it. All the work and long hours I put into getting it ready and it just sat there. I had planned on staying in Seattle for a few more weeks until my phone beeped with a text message from Gretchen.

"Giselle went into labor and she's in the hospital. It's way too early, Lily. Things aren't looking good. She's asking for you."

"I'm on the next flight out. Tell her I'm on my way."

I couldn't believe Giselle was in labor. She still had eight weeks left and we hadn't even had her baby shower yet. I called the airlines and booked the next flight out, which would get me into Los Angeles around eight p.m. I quickly threw all my things in my suitcase and drove to the airport. My mother and Brynn weren't home, so I sent them a text message explaining why I had to suddenly leave and go back to Santa Monica. As I sat on the plane, I couldn't stop fidgeting. Not only was I scared for Giselle, I was a nervous wreck to see Luke. When the plane finally landed, I walked to my car and drove straight to the hospital.

As the elevator doors opened, Lucky was standing there. I stepped off and gave him a tight hug.

"How is she?" I asked.

He looked different. He had a look of worry and despair on his face that I'd never seen before, a seriousness that made me worry even more.

"She's scared and so am I. Thank you for coming back, Lily. She's been asking for you. I've never seen her like this. She's always so strong and sure of everything. But now, she's really scared and nervous."

"Don't worry. I'm sure everything will be fine. I'll go see her now. Where are you heading?"

"To grab something to eat. Do you want anything?" he asked.

"No. I'm good." I smiled as I patted his shoulder.

I walked down to Giselle's room, and when I opened the door, she looked up at me and started crying. My problems suddenly disappeared and my main focus was my best friend, who needed me. I tilted my head and walked over to her bed, sitting down on the edge and giving her a hug with tears in my eyes.

"I'm so happy you're back," she cried. "Lily, I'm so worried. The doctors aren't sure what's going to happen.

They're running all kinds of tests and put me on some medication."

"Shh. The doctors know what they're doing and the baby is going to be fine." I smiled.

Gretchen reached over and grabbed my hand.

"Welcome home." She smiled.

"Where's Lucky?" Giselle asked.

"He went to get something to eat. He'll be back soon. He better be treating you right," I said.

"He is. He's so worried," she said as she closed her eyes.

Gretchen motioned for me to step to the other side of the room.

"Thank you for coming. I know this has to be so hard for you right now and I'm sorry," she whispered.

"Don't worry about me. I'm fine. The three of us have been through so much together and I would never not be here for either one of you," I said as I hugged her.

Lucky walked back in the room and went right over to Giselle's bedside. I stood there and watched him as he held her hand and gently rubbed his thumb back and forth across her skin.

"I'm going to get some coffee," I said.

"The coffee bar is closed now, but there's a machine down the hall. Believe it or not, the coffee is pretty good," Gretchen said.

As I stepped out of the room, I looked to my left and saw Luke standing a few feet away. I started to tremble and my heart began to beat at a rapid pace. All I kept hearing in my head was our conversation and how he said he blamed me for Callie's death. I turned away and walked down the hall towards the coffee machine. I prayed he didn't follow me. The rapid beating of my heart ached so badly that I felt like I was having a heart attack. I turned to the right and into the small waiting room that housed the coffee machine.

"Lily, please don't turn away from me," he said from behind.

I put my money in the machine with a shaking hand and hit the coffee button.

"I have nothing to say to you, Luke. I'm back for Giselle."

"I know, babe."

I turned around and looked at him as I held up my finger. "Don't. Don't call me that. You lost that right. I'm not doing this with you. I have my best friend lying in a hospital bed, ready to give birth two months early, and that's what I'm focusing on."

I grabbed the cup from the machine and stormed past him. I heard him yell my name, but I didn't care. I couldn't care. Because if I did, I'd fall to pieces yet once again.

****

Luke

I sat down in the chair and cupped my face in my hands. She hated me. I could see it in her eyes and I didn't blame her one bit.

"Bro, are you okay?" Sam said as he sat down next to me.

"No," I replied as I looked up at him. "I saw Lily and she ran from me."

"What did you expect? The last time the two of you spoke, you said some awful things to her."

"I know that and I'm trying to apologize to her, but she won't let me."

"She will, in time."

"I don't have time, Sam. I need to make things right, now!"

"Come on," he said as he put his hand on my shoulder. "Let's go see how Lucky and Giselle are doing."

I didn't know if that was such a good idea because Lily was in the room. But, Lucky and Giselle were both my good friends and I needed to make sure everything was going to be okay. Sam and I walked into the room and my eyes went straight to Lily, who was sitting on the edge of the bed, holding Giselle's hand. She knew we walked in but refused to turn around and look at us.

"Hey, Lily." Sam smiled as he walked over to her and kissed her cheek.

"Hi, Sam," she replied.

"Welcome home."

"Thank you."

Lucky walked over to me and Sam and asked us if we could step outside with him. He took us out to a courtyard and then pulled a cigarette from his pocket.

"Dude, when did you start smoking again?" Sam asked.

"Since all of this. I'm scared, guys. This is my baby, my daughter, we're talking about and not knowing anything is driving me crazy. I'm ready to punch someone."

"You need to stay calm for Giselle's and your daughter's sake," I said.

"I know I do. It's hard though. Thanks, guys, for coming to the hospital. It means a lot to us."

Lucky wasn't being typical Lucky anymore. He was legitimately scared and he had every reason to be. He was acting like a responsible adult. As soon as he finished his smoke, we went back up to the room, where the nurse told all of us that visiting hours were over for everyone except Lucky. I watched as Lily gave Giselle a kiss on the cheek and told her that she'd be back in the morning, and I also watched her walk right out the door without even looking at me and possibly right out of my life.

"Luke, she needs time," Gretchen said as she put her hand on my arm.

"Everybody keeps telling me that," I said as I walked out of the room.

Chapter 17

Lily

Just as I parked the Explorer and grabbed my suitcase from the back, Luke's Jeep pulled up. Shit. I pulled up the handle on my suitcase and began rolling it to the door. I heard his car door shut and, suddenly, his hand was grabbing my suitcase.

"Let me help you, Lily," he said.

"I can do it myself," I snapped as I jerked the suitcase away from him.

"Hate me! Hate me all you want because I'm sorry for everything!" he yelled. "I'm sorry for what I said to you. I want you, Lily. I want our relationship back. I love you!"

I stopped walking when I heard his words and let the rage build inside me. I turned around in a fit of anger and looked at him underneath the bright street light.

"You think you can just come back to town when you're ready and expect things to go back to normal? You broke me. You shattered me when you stood there and said you blamed me for Callie's death. You crushed me into even more tiny pieces when you walked out and left me. You, Luke Matthews, did that to me!" I screamed.

By that time, I was a sobbing mess and that was when Gretchen and Sam pulled up. "We needed each other for support, and you turned your back on me. You wouldn't even listen to me, and for that, I hate you! Do you hear me? There is no 'us.' You broke us way beyond repair!" I screamed.

Gretchen came running over and hugged me as tightly as she could. She grabbed my suitcase, the keys out of my hand, and led me into my apartment.

"Who the hell does he think he is?" I cried.

She walked into the kitchen and pulled a bottle of wine from the cabinet. She poured some in a glass and handed it to me, then went into the bathroom and grabbed some tissues.

"Here," she said as she handed them to me.

I sat down on the couch and brought my knees up to my chest.

"Lily, I'm really worried about you."

"Don't be. I just exploded. He had it coming. You better get back to Sam. I'll call you in the morning."

"I don't want to leave you."

"Go. Please. I love you but I need to be alone."

She leaned over and kissed my forehead. "You better call me first thing in the morning."

"I will. Thank you, Gretchen."

"I'm so happy you're back," she said as she hugged me.

****

Luke

She made it very clear that she didn't want anything to do with me. I fucked up in such a way that I didn't know how the hell to fix it. Gretchen walked into the apartment and looked at me. She stood there with an angry look on her face and shook her finger at me, but the words wouldn't come out of her mouth.

"Don't, Gretchen. I already know," I said with a tear in my eye as I looked down.

Sam was sitting at the table, not saying a word. Gretchen walked over to me and wrapped her arms around me.

"I love you, Luke. You're my friend just as much as Lily is. You're both hurting in such a way that I feel so helpless."

"I need her back. I want her back. She won't listen to me and I don't know what to do."

"I think the best thing you can do is slowly try to rebuild your friendship. She can't hate you forever. I know she won't. I think it's just the shock of seeing you again after so many weeks. She'll calm down and, when she does, she'll need you. I know Lily and you're the best thing in her life and she'll come to realize that once she calms down."

Sam walked over to us and wrapped his arms around both of us.

"Yeah, what she said."

I couldn't help but let out a soft laugh. Gretchen was right. It was time to focus on winning Lily back and that was what I was going to do, no matter what the cost was. And now it wasn't only Lily I needed to win back, I also needed to win back Charley.

****

Lily

The next morning, I got up at the crack of dawn and was going to go to the studio before I headed to the hospital to see Giselle. I had just finished getting dressed when my phone rang. I picked it up and saw Lucky was calling.

"Hello," I answered.

"Lily, Giselle is in labor and the doctors say she has to deliver the baby. She's asking for you. She wants you in the delivery room."

"Tell her I'm on my way."

I put on my shoes and grabbed my keys. As soon as I got in the Explorer, I inserted the key and turned it. It wouldn't start. FUCK! *Come on, come on*, I said as I tried multiple times. I started pounding the steering wheel with my fists when I saw Luke walk out of the building. I got out of the SUV and had no choice but to ask him if Sam and Gretchen were still home.

"Is Sam or Gretchen still home?" I asked with an attitude.

"No. They went to breakfast."

I was fidgeting again and a nervous wreck, but I had to put Giselle and the baby first.

"Lucky called and Giselle is in labor."

"I know. He just called me. I'm heading there now. The Explorer won't start, will it?" he asked.

"No."

"Get in my Jeep. I'll drive you there."

I took in a deep breath. This was not supposed to happen. I had no choice but to go with him. I climbed in the Jeep, fastened my seat belt, and looked out the passenger window.

"Lily—"

I put up my hand to stop him. "No words. Just get me to the hospital."

He sighed and sped off out of the parking lot. The ride there was silent. I wouldn't look at him. I couldn't look at him because, if I did, I'd break down again. He dropped me off at the door and I ran up to Giselle's room. When I walked in, she was yelling in pain. Lucky was putting a cool cloth on her head and holding one hand, while Gretchen was holding the other.

"Lily," Giselle cried. "It's too early. I can't have her yet. It's too early."

"Shh. It's going to be all right. I promise," I said as I ran my hand across her hair.

I looked at Gretchen. "Why did you and Sam have to go to breakfast so early? The Explorer wouldn't start and I had to get a ride in with Luke. Do you know how uncomfortable that was?"

"Sorry, but we were hungry," she said. You really need to get a new car."

Giselle yelled with another contraction. The doctor walked back in the room and told her that it was time to start pushing. She was crying and telling the doctor that it was too early. Lucky was trying to soothe her and make her comfortable. Finally, after talking to her and helping her through it, she delivered her baby girl.

"We need to take her to the neonatal unit right away," the nurse said with sympathy as she held the baby to her.

"Can I just touch her?" Giselle asked as she cried.

The nurse brought the baby closer to her and Lucky. He kissed her lightly on the head and Giselle touched her tiny hand. The nurse took her out of the room immediately and Giselle began to sob uncontrollably. Lucky did his best to calm her down. We thought it would be best for the two of them, as parents, to be left alone. Gretchen and I walked out of the room and saw Sam and Luke sitting in the waiting room across the hall. Gretchen went over to them and I walked down to the coffee bar.

I took my coffee outside to the courtyard and took a seat on a wrought-iron bench. I looked at my phone. I had a text message from my mom.

"Just checking in and making sure you're okay."

"I'm as good as I can be. Giselle had the baby about thirty minutes ago and we're not sure what's going to happen."

"I'm sorry, Lily. Girls are strong. That baby of hers is going to be just fine."

"Thanks, Mom. I'll talk to you soon."

I took a sip of my coffee and then looked down at the ground.

"Hey," Luke said.

I closed my eyes and was ready to lash out at him and tell him to get the fuck away from me, but I didn't have the strength. So I just looked up at him with sad eyes.

"The baby is going to be okay," he said.

"You don't know that for sure. There are so many complications for a baby born prematurely."

"Do you mind if I sit down?"

I put my hand out, signaling that I really had no choice because there were other people in the courtyard and I didn't want to cause a scene. He sat there with his elbows on his knees and his face cupped in his hands.

Chapter 18

Lily

"I can take a look at your car and see what's wrong," Luke said.

"Nah. I'll have it towed again. I don't need your help," I snapped quietly.

"I know you don't, but I want to help."

I turned my head and looked at him. "You really want to help me? You can do that by leaving me alone," I said as I shook my head and tears stung my eyes.

I got up from the bench and walked back into the hospital. I couldn't escape the pain that constantly flowed throughout my body, the gut-wrenching pain that was such a huge part of my life. I walked into Giselle's room and sat down next to her, grabbing her hand.

"The doctor said that her lungs aren't fully mature yet and they have her on a breathing machine. He said the next twenty-four hours are critical, but he's optimistic that she'll pull through."

"Of course she'll pull through. She's a girl. A strong girl who comes from a line of strong women like her mom." I smiled.

"She is strong, isn't she?"

"She sure is," I said. "Have you picked a name for her yet?"

"Yeah, we did." She smiled as she looked at Lucky.

"Isabella Grace Chambers," Lucky replied.

"That's a beautiful name. You look tired, Giselle. You better get some rest. I'm going to head out unless you want me to stay."

"No. You go do what you have to do. I'll see you later."

I kissed her and Lucky on the cheek and walked over to the neonatal unit. Luke was standing there, looking through the window. I took in a deep breath as I walked up and stood next to him.

"She's so tiny," he said.

"Yeah, she is. She'll be okay. I know she will."

Luke looked over at me and then back at Isabella.

"Look, I'm sorry for snapping at you today. Last night, no. Today, yes."

"I don't blame you. How are you getting home or wherever you have to go?"

"I was going to catch a ride with Sam or Gretchen, but I can't find them."

"They left already. Sam said he had to go to work and Gretchen had something to do."

"That's great. I'll call a cab then."

"I can drive you home, Lily," he replied as he still stared straight ahead.

"Don't you have to get to the bar?" I asked.

"The bar can wait."

"Thanks," I softly said.

"Are you ready now?" he asked.

"Yeah. I guess I'll go home and call a tow truck."

I followed behind him out of the hospital and into the Jeep. A part of me wanted to reach over and hold his hand, but the bigger part of me wanted to hit him.

****

Luke

As soon as we pulled into the parking lot of the apartment building, Lily got out and climbed into her Explorer to try and start it one last time before she called the tow truck. She looked at me when it suddenly started.

"What the hell!" she exclaimed.

I shrugged my shoulders. That was weird that it just started after it wouldn't turn over this morning. I climbed back in my Jeep and drove to the bar. I decided that I had no choice but to respect Lily's wishes and leave her alone. I could see the pain that resided in her eyes because it was same pain as mine.

"Hey," Maddie said as I walked in the bar.

"Hey. Giselle had the baby."

"Is she okay?" she asked.

"The next twenty-four hours are critical, but I think she'll pull through. How's Charley? I sent her a couple of text messages and she won't respond."

"She really wants nothing to do with you."

I rolled my eyes and sighed. "She's not the only one."

"Have you talked to Lily yet?"

"You mean have I been screamed at and been told that she hates me and that I broke her? Yes."

"Aw, Luke. I'm sorry."

"I don't want to talk about it anymore," I said as I walked to my office.

Cody was sitting at my desk again and it looked like she was going over the books.

"Hey, Luke. I'll be done in a second."

"Hey. I really need to have another office built," I said as I turned and walked out.

I pulled my phone from my pocket and sent Lily a text message.

"Hey, I'm really sorry to bother you, but do you still have the phone number for that contractor you used for your studio?"

A few minutes later, her reply came through with only his name and phone number. What the hell did I expect? I dialed the number and waited for him to answer.

"Hello, Cameron Cole here."

Sandi Lynn

"Cameron, my name is Luke Matthews. I got your number from Lily Gilmore. You did some work on her photography studio."

"Hi, Luke. What can I do for you?"

"I own a bar and was looking to have a small office built for my assistant."

"Sure. I can come by later this afternoon, take a look, and give you an estimate if you're going to be around."

"Sounds great, Cameron. I'll be here."

I gave him the address and he knew exactly where it was. I walked behind the bar and started drying off the rack of glasses that were sitting there.

"Cameron, a contractor, will be stopping by later to look at building an office for Cody," I said to Maddie.

"Oh. So you plan on keeping her around?"

"Don't start with me, Maddie. She's a good employee."

"I have a feeling that we're going to see how good she really is," she said as she walked away.

I rolled my eyes as I placed the dry glasses on the shelf. I looked up and saw Cody walking across the bar in her short skirt and tight shirt. She perched herself on the barstool and showed me some figures on a report.

"See these numbers? This is your profit and this is your loss. They almost equal out. So technically, you really didn't make any money last month."

"That's nice to know," I sighed.

119

"Don't sweat it. We'll get you up there so you're rolling in the dough. I remembered that you mentioned bringing in other bands to play on the weekends. I think you should do Friday, Saturday, and Sundays."

"I know. I've already thought of that and I'm going to do it. I just haven't had the time to contact any bands or listen to them."

"I have an idea." She smiled as she placed her hand on my arm. "I'm going to place an ad online. I know of a few sites that a lot of bands visit and the ad will grab their attention."

"Thanks, Cody. I'm sorry that I haven't been here much for you since you started. It's just with Lily and all the shit going on—"

"Luke, I understand. Don't worry about it." She smiled. "Remember, I'm here if you ever want to talk."

I gave her a smile and looked up when the bar door opened.

"Luke Matthews?" the guy asked as he walked towards me.

"Yep, that's me," I answered as I held out my hand.

"I'm Cameron Cole."

"Great to meet you, Cameron. Follow me and I'll show you where I was thinking about putting the office."

He followed me to the back and I showed him the space. He looked around, stood back, took out his measuring tape, and nodded his head.

"Okay. This will work." He smiled.

We stood and talked for quite a while. Lily had told me how nice he was and she was right. He was a great guy and he knew his stuff.

"I have a job that'll be finished up in a couple of days. I can start then."

"Sounds good, man," I said as I held out my hand. "Thank you for coming out."

"No problem. Tell Lily I said hi. She's a great photographer."

I gave a small smile. "Yeah, she is."

As he left the bar, Cody walked over to me with a smile on her face.

"What's the verdict?"

"You'll have your own office soon."

She looped her arm around mine and laid her head on my shoulder.

"Thanks, but I really don't mind sharing with you. You can tuck me in a corner and I'll be just as happy."

I looked up and noticed Sam walking towards me. Cody immediately let go of my arm and walked away.

"What the fuck was that, Luke? Are you already giving up on Lily and moving on?"

"Hell no. She was just thanking me for the new office I'm having built so she doesn't have to share mine. Jesus Christ, man. You can fuck off for even thinking that."

"Really, bro, because what if it was Lily who walked back here instead of me?"

"Well, I don't have to worry about that, do I? She won't even speak to me, let alone walk into my bar," I said as I walked away and punched the wall.

"Are you going to the hospital later?" he asked.

"Yeah. I want to bring Giselle some flowers."

"Good idea. I'll talk to you later," he said as he started to walk away.

"Sam," I called. "Why did you come by the bar?"

"Oh, I was going to talk to you about something, but it can wait."

"Are you sure? You're already here."

"I'm sure. We'll talk later." He smiled.

Chapter 19

Lily

I stepped inside my apartment and threw my keys on the counter. I'd been at the studio, doing the final clean up because I decided that I was going to open within the next couple of days. Now that I was back, I needed to focus on something other than Luke. I jumped into the shower, cleaned up, and put on fresh clothes before I headed to the hospital. As I locked up my apartment, Luke walked out of his. My heart felt like it going to jump out of my throat.

"Hey," he said without looking at me.

"Hey," I replied and then walked to the Explorer.

I climbed in and tried not to watch Luke get in his Jeep, but my eyes couldn't help it. I put the key in the ignition and nothing. Luke drove off and I was about ready have a breakdown. I turned the key again. Nothing. My phone rang and it was Luke.

"Hello," I answered softly.

"The Explorer won't start again, will it?"

"Nope," I said quietly because I was going to lose it any second.

"I'm back," he said as he hung up and pulled up next to me.

I rolled down my window and looked at him.

"Are you going to the hospital?" he asked.

"Yeah."

"Me too. Hop in," he said with a small smile.

For fuck's sake. You have got to be kidding me. I grabbed my purse and climbed into the Jeep.

"We have to stop at the florist first. I want to pick up some flowers for Giselle," he said.

I nodded my head. "Okay."

I kept my head turned and looked out the passenger window. Luke pulled into the parking lot of the florist and we both went inside. I wanted to get some balloons for Giselle and Lucky. Luke stood in front of the cooler, looking at the pink roses. He told the sales lady that he'd take a dozen while I had another sales lady blow up a few balloons. This was awkward and, first thing tomorrow morning, I was having the Explorer towed and looking for a new vehicle. As soon as we got back in the Jeep, Luke asked me if I would mind holding the roses. I took them from him and continued to look out the window.

"I met Cameron Cole today," he said out of the clear blue.

"Really?" I asked.

"Yeah. He's going to build a small office for Cody."

"That's nice."

"He's a really nice guy. I can see why you liked him so much."

"Yep. He's great."

I heard him sigh and then there was silence until he asked me about Charley.

"Have you seen Charley yet?"

"No. I was planning on seeing her tomorrow."

"She told me she hated me."

"Why would she say that?" I asked as I looked at him.

"Because you left."

"I'm sure she didn't mean it. You know how kids are."

That little girl meant everything to him and it must have killed him to hear her say that. I didn't stop to think how she would be affected by what happened between me and Luke and now I felt like total shit. Worse than I already did. He pulled into a parking space at the hospital and we went up to Giselle's room. Luke walked over, gave her a kiss, and handed her the beautiful pink roses. I looked over at Gretchen and Sam, who were staring at each other when Luke and I walked in. I handed Lucky the balloons and took a seat on the edge of the bed.

"How's she doing?" I asked.

"So far, she's doing well. The doctor is really optimistic. We got to sit with her earlier. It's so hard to see her hooked up to all those monitors and that breathing machine." She began to cry.

I leaned over and hugged her. "I know, but it's helping her. Just remember that. Pretty soon, you'll be holding her in your arms and this will all be behind you."

Lucky, Luke, and Sam stepped out of the room and Gretchen walked over and sat down in the chair by us.

"Did you come here with Luke? What's going on?"

"The damn Explorer was dead again and Luke was leaving to come here, so he offered me a ride."

"That's the second time today, Lily," Gretchen said.

"No shit, and I can't believe it."

"Have the two of you talked?" Giselle asked.

"You mean besides Lily screaming at him last night in the middle of the parking lot?"

I shot Gretchen a look. "Very little and nothing but small talk. I told him this morning to leave me alone."

Giselle took hold of my hand. "Sweetie, don't you think that maybe you should listen to him? Hear what he has to say."

"He said all I needed to hear that night he accused me of killing Callie and left. It's obvious he isn't over her and I don't think he'll ever be."

"That's not true," Sam said as he walked back in the room.

"Sam, I'm not talking about this anymore."

"Where's Lucky?" Giselle asked.

"He and Luke are looking at Isabella. She's a beauty, Giselle. Thank God she looks like you." He laughed.

We all laughed and it felt good. It felt good to be in the company of my best friends at a time I needed them most. When Luke and Lucky walked back in the room, I walked out and headed for the coffee machine. I pulled my phone from my pocket and sent Maddie a text message.

"Hi. Would it be okay if I pick Charley up from school tomorrow and take her to the studio with me for a while?"

"Sure. She'll love that. She misses you so much and so do I."

"I miss you both too. Don't tell her that I'm picking her up. I want it to be a surprise."

****

Luke

I didn't know if following Lily out of the room was a good idea, but I didn't care. I just wanted to be where she was. I took some change out of my pocket and walked into the waiting room with the coffee machine.

"Excuse me," I said as Lily was looking at her phone and standing in front of the machine.

"Sorry," she said as she moved out of the way.

I put the change in the machine and pressed the button for a cup of black coffee.

"Is this stuff any good?" I asked her.

"It's no Starbucks, that's for sure. But it's pretty decent."

She left the waiting room and I followed behind. We walked back into Giselle's room and noticed that Sam and Gretchen were gone.

"Where did they go?" Lily asked Giselle.

"They left. They said they had something they had to do and they'll be back tomorrow."

"Great. I was going to get a ride home with them."

"Why? Luke's here. He'll drive you home. Right?" Lucky smiled.

"Of course," I said.

"Anyway, I'm really tired. Thank you for the flowers and the balloons." Giselle smiled.

"You're welcome." I walked over and gave her a kiss goodbye.

Lily and I walked out of the room and I turned and looked at her.

"Did we just get kicked out?"

"Yeah. I think we did." She smiled.

God, it was good to see her smile again. I wanted to run my hand down her cheek and tell her how much I loved her, but at the risk of getting slapped, I kept my hands to myself and my mouth shut.

"I can't believe Gretchen and Sam took off like that," she said.

"I know. They did that this morning too."

"The least they could've done was tell us," Lily said.

We climbed in my Jeep and, as we pulled out of the parking lot, I had a thought. A thought that would really piss Lily off, but at this point, I didn't care.

"I'm sorry, Lily, but I'm starving and I need to grab something to eat."

"NOW?!" she exclaimed.

"Yeah. I haven't eaten all day. We can just stop at that diner up the street. It's two minutes from here."

"Just drive thru a McDonalds or something and eat it in your apartment."

"The closest McDonalds is three miles from here," I said as I pulled into the parking lot of the diner. "See? We're already here."

She looked at me and rolled her eyes.

"Listen, I promise I won't talk to you. But I'm driving and I'm starving, and I'm getting something to eat before I drive you home."

"Whatever," she said as she opened and then slammed the door shut.

We walked into the diner. She was pissed. I was going to take advantage of any opportunity I had to be alone with her.

Chapter 20

Lily

The nerve of him. We were seated in a booth and I looked around to see if there was another one available. Another booth just for me.

"Are you looking to sit somewhere else?" he asked.

Damn him. I hated that he knew me too well in these types of situations.

"Yes. Yes, I am because this is bullshit that you brought me here," I said through gritted teeth across the table.

I picked up my menu and held it up to my face so he couldn't see me. This wasn't right and it was not helping my state of mind.

"I'm sorry, Lily. You're right. Let's go," he said as he got up from the booth.

I took in a deep breath. Every piece of me wanted to get up from my seat and follow him, but I couldn't.

"Sit down and look at the menu," I said.

"No, seriously. Let's go. I can't do this with you either. I thought I could, but I can't."

"You're making a scene, Luke. Sit down and let's order dinner."

He sighed, sat back down, and opened his menu. The waitress walked over and took our drink order. Since this place didn't have alcohol, I just ordered coffee. Luke stuck with water. I picked up my phone and sent a text message to Gretchen.

"Thanks a lot for leaving the hospital without giving me a ride home."

"Sorry. We sort of forgot you didn't drive. But Luke was there. He gave you a ride home, right?"

"Not yet. He was starving, so he stopped at a diner to get something to eat."

"Oh. Well, use this time to talk to him."

"Goodbye, Gretchen."

"Are you bitching to Gretchen about having to stop here?"

DAMN. HIM. "No. I was—It's none of your business."

The waitress came back with our drinks and took our order. I only ordered a side salad because I wasn't hungry, but I didn't want Luke to start in on me. The couple sitting at the table next to us were being overly affectionate. They were holding hands across the table, stealing little kisses, smiling, laughing, and being what Luke and I used to be like. I could feel the tears spring to my eyes. The waitress brought our food just in time.

"I saw you staring at that couple over there," he said as he took a bite of his burger.

"I wasn't staring."

"They remind me of two other people."

"Really? Because nothing's really as it seems. They'll wake up one day."

He took another bite of his burger and stared at me while nodding his head. That was the end of our conversation for the rest of the night. After we finished eating, Luke drove back to the apartment. I walked in mine, and he walked in his without as much as a goodnight.

****

Luke

I walked in my apartment and threw my keys on the table. Sam and Gretchen were snuggled on the couch, watching a movie.

"Hey, what took you so long to get back?" Sam asked.

"Before coming home, I stopped off and got something to eat."

"Wasn't Lily with you?"

"Yeah, she was, and it didn't go so well. It's over between me and Lily. I can't do it anymore. She won't even listen to me. She won't talk about that night and she won't let me explain. It's over, so stop trying to push us together."

"What are you talking about?" Sam asked.

"I suspect the two of you had something to do with Lily's SUV not starting. I started piecing some things together the second time it happened. Thanks, but no thanks," I said as I walked to my room.

"We were only trying to help you two out," Sam yelled.

I heard my phone beep and I pulled it out of my pocket. I had a text message from Cody.

"Hi, Luke. I just wanted you to know that I posted the ad for band auditions and there's already about twenty bands that want to play at the bar."

I smiled. *"Thanks, Cody. I appreciate your hard work. Now stop thinking about business and take the night off."*

"I'm just sitting at home with nothing to do. No big deal."

"I appreciate it. Good night."

"Good night, Luke."

I took off my t-shirt and lay down on the bed with my hands behind my head. I thought about what Sam and Gretchen had done to try and get me and Lily alone. I needed to tell her because she was going to have the Explorer towed tomorrow and possibly go buy a new one.

"Sorry to bother you, but I thought you should know that Sam and Gretchen were responsible for the Explorer not starting today. They were scheming to try and get us alone. You won't need to have it towed tomorrow."

"Real special friends. Thanks for letting me know."

What I wouldn't have given right then to be in her bed with my arms wrapped tightly around her. I missed her touch, her smell, the softness of her hair, and her beautiful smile. I was desperate to run my hand gently up and down her silky skin and I was desperate to hear her soft moans when my fingers went deep inside her. Shit. I was getting hard.

Lily

I didn't sleep anymore. I was lucky if I could get in three hours' worth. I was back to where I was two years ago after I left Seattle. My mind wouldn't settle down with thoughts of Luke, and my anger still consumed me. I rolled out of bed and took a hot shower. I couldn't believe that Sam and Gretchen would do such a thing, especially knowing how I felt. I got dressed, grabbed my coffee, and, when I opened the door, I saw Charley coming down the stairs. She looked at me, threw her backpack down, and ran to me, throwing her arms around my legs.

"Lily!"

"Hi, baby," I said as I hugged her. "How are you?"

"I knew you'd come back."

"Of course. I just went to visit my mom and my sister in Seattle."

Luke walked out of his apartment and looked at us.

"Uncle Luke, did you know that Lily's back?"

He smiled at her as he patted her head. "Yeah, I knew, peanut."

She could tell something was up because neither one of us said a word to each other. She looked at him and then at me as Maddie came walking down the stairs.

"What's wrong? Why aren't the two of you talking?" she asked.

"Come on, Charley. You're going to be late for school," Maddie said.

I bent down and placed my hand on her cheek. "Guess what. I'm picking you up today and taking you to my new studio. I need some help and I couldn't think of a more qualified person to help me."

"Really!"

"Yes." I smiled. "Now go to school. I'll see you later."

She gave me a kiss on the cheek, gave Luke a dirty look, and then walked out the building door. I locked up my apartment and Luke walked out.

I stopped by the hospital on my way to the studio to see how Giselle and the baby were doing. When I walked in, she was eating breakfast.

"Just in time. Would you like some of this crap they claim is oatmeal?" she asked.

"No thanks. I'm good." I smiled as I sat down in the chair next to her bed. "How is Isabella doing?"

"She's doing great. The doctor said that she'll probably be ready to go home in a couple of weeks. Lucky and I got to hold her last night and we both cried. I can't wait for my parents to meet her; they're flying in today. I told Lucky he better be on his best behavior or else. The last time they were here, after Gretchen's accident, they weren't impressed with him."

"Speaking of Lucky, where is he?"

"Right here." He smiled as he walked into the room, holding a brown bag. "I bring real food."

He walked over to me and gave me a kiss on the head. I got up from the chair and hugged Giselle.

"I'm going to go. I need to head over to the studio."

"Oh, I forgot to tell you. Adalynn over at *Prim* wants you to give her a call. She wants to talk to you about doing a photo shoot for the magazine. She saw the pictures of Rory and the girls and was really impressed."

"Seriously?"

"Yeah, so call her today. This could be a huge opportunity for you."

I leaned over and kissed her cheek. "Thank you. I'll call her as soon as I get to the studio. Bye, Lucky."

"Bye, babe. Hey, do me a favor."

"What is it?" I asked.

"Talk to Luke. He misses you in a really bad way."

"Then he shouldn't have said what he did. I love you both. I'll see you later," I said as I walked out of the room.

As soon as I got to the studio, I dialed Adalynn over at *Prim*.

"This is Adalynn," she answered.

"Hi, Adalynn. It's Lily Gilmore. Giselle said that you wanted me to give you a call."

"Oh yes, Lily. How are you?"

"I'm good. How are you?"

"Doing great. I was hoping that you'd be available to do a photo shoot for a fall fashion spread I'm doing for next month's issue of *Prim*."

"I would be honored. Thank you."

"I saw the pictures you took of Rory and my sweet girls and the way you captured their emotions was really good. I especially loved the sensual pictures you took of Rory."

"She showed you those?"

"Yes, and so did Ian. He was blown away and wouldn't stop raving about you and your work. If you're available, I would like to do the shoot in a couple of days. I want some shots on the Santa Monica Pier and then at your studio would be great."

"Sounds good. I'm available whenever you need me."

"Great. Let's meet at the pier at noon. I'll have a meeting with the models and tell them it's a go."

"Thank you, Adalynn. I really appreciate you giving me this opportunity."

"No problem. I'll see you Friday."

I couldn't believe it. For the first time in a long time, excitement shot throughout my body. Shit. I was going to need an assistant. There was no way I could do that shoot on my own with all that equipment. How was I going to find someone on such short notice? I decided to call Sam with the hopes that maybe he knew someone who would be interested.

"Hey, Lils," he answered.

"Hey, Sam. Do you know anyone who's looking for a job as a photographer's assistant?"

"No, I don't. Why?"

"I'm doing my first photo shoot in a couple of days for *Prim* magazine and I need an assistant. I thought maybe you'd know someone around your firm or someone who knows someone."

"Sorry. But why don't you call the art department over at UCLA? I'm sure there are college students who are in the photography program that would love to do that."

"Great idea. I didn't even think about that. Thanks, Sam. Oh, by the way, you and Gretchen aren't off the hook about the little stunt you two pulled with my truck."

"Oh. You know about that? Sorry."

"Yeah, I know and I'm not happy, but we'll talk about it later."

"Okay. I'll warn Gretchen," he sighed.

I was really happy about Sam's suggestion to call UCLA. I googled the number and dialed their art department. The director, Mr. Smith, seemed really nice and told me to come right over because he had the perfect person for me. L.A. traffic was the worst. What should have taken me fifteen minutes to get to UCLA, took me an hour. I found my way to the art department and met Mr. Smith. When we reached the photography room, he introduced me to a guy named Wyatt. He was a second-year photography student and one of the best in his class.

"Wyatt, I would like you to meet Lily Gilmore. She's the photographer I was telling you about."

"Nice to meet you, Miss Gilmore." He smiled as he held out his hand.

"Please call me Lily. It's nice to meet you too."

"I'll leave you two alone to get acquainted." Mr. Smith smiled.

Chapter 21

Luke

I was sitting at my desk, going over some invoices, when Cody walked into the office.

"Hey, Luke."

"Hey," I replied without looking up.

"The first band will be here in a couple of hours to audition."

"Okay."

"Are you okay?" she asked.

Am I okay? No, I wasn't, but I wasn't going to let her know that. I wasn't sure I'd ever be okay again unless I got Lily back.

"Yeah, I'm fine. I just have a lot on my mind."

She gave me a small smile and walked out of the office. A few moments later, there was a knock on my door. I looked up and saw my mom and dad standing there, smiling at me.

"Mom, Dad, you're back. How was your trip?" I asked as I got up and hugged them.

"It was marvelous." My mom smiled.

"How are you, son?" my dad asked as we lightly hugged.

"I'm good."

"I'm having Charley's birthday party this weekend at the house, so you and Lily better not have other plans. I'm excited to see her. How is she?"

Shit. Shit. Shit. How would I tell my parents that we weren't together anymore and that I royally fucked things up?

"Let's go take a seat and have some lunch. I have something to tell you."

"Now you're worrying me, Luke," my mom said.

I told Maddie to join us, but she said that I needed to talk to our parents alone. We took a seat at the table and ordered some lunch.

"Something happened while you were gone. Lily and I broke up."

I watched as tears sprang to my mother's eyes. "Why?"

"Son, I'm sorry," my dad said.

"It was all my fault and now she hates me. I found out something about her. I was in shock. I accused her of something horrible and I took off for a while. When I came back, she was gone. Now she's back because our friend had her baby and Lily won't talk to me or let me explain."

The sad look on my mother's face broke my heart. She reached over and placed her hand on mine.

"What did she do?"

"Remember when Callie and I were in Portland for the weekend and I told you that a woman came up to us at the restaurant and gave us those tickets to Aruba?"

"Yes."

"That woman was Lily, but neither one of us remembered each other because it had been a little over year."

She slowly slid her hand off of mine and glared at me.

"What exactly are you saying, Luke?" my dad asked.

Before I could get any words out of my mouth, my mother spoke. "I think he's trying to tell us that he blamed Lily for the accident."

"That's ridiculous. She didn't cause the accident."

"I know that. But when I first found out, I was in shock and I told her that if she wouldn't have given us the tickets, then Callie would still be alive."

"Oh Luke," my mother said as a tear ran down her cheek.

Maddie walked over and clasped her shoulders. "He's trying to win her back, Mom."

"I went and rented a cabin from Pastor Joe and we had a long talk. He made me realize some things. I'm so sorry, Mom and Dad."

My dad reached over and gave my arm a light squeeze while my mom got up from her seat and hugged me.

"She'll come around. Lily loves you too much to give up. She just needs time."

"I hope so, Mom, because I don't think I can live without her."

Cody walked over to let me know that the first band was here. I had them set up on the stage and then I sat back with my parents and watched them perform.

****

Lily

"I like you, Wyatt, and I think we'll work well together. You're hired." I smiled.

"Thank you, Lily. I'm so excited."

Wyatt's passion for photography was what drew me to him. Listening to the way he felt about photographs and art reminded me so much of myself. I took a look at some of his photos and was very impressed. He still had a lot to learn, so working for me would be perfect for him.

"Who is this fine, ripped-looking man?" I asked as I studied the black and white photograph.

"That's my boyfriend, Grant. He's trying to break into the modeling biz."

"Well, it looks to me like he should have no problem."

"He is a hottie, isn't he?" Wyatt smiled.

I looked at the clock on the wall. It was almost time for Charley to get out of school. If I didn't leave now, I would be late.

"Why don't you stop by my studio tomorrow after classes and we can go over a few things before Friday's shoot."

"I will be there! Thank you for this amazing opportunity, Lily," Wyatt said as he hugged me goodbye.

I drove to the school to pick up Charley. I made it just in time, as I saw her walking out the doors when I pulled up. A huge smile graced her face as she climbed in the Explorer and hugged me.

"How was school?" I asked.

"It was okay. I couldn't wait for it to be over so I could go with you to your studio. I'm so excited to see it."

As we stepped through the door, Charley looked around at all the pictures on the wall.

"I like your pictures, but you don't have one in this spot and it looks weird," she said as she pointed to the corner.

"That's because I was saving that spot for someone special."

She looked up at me and smiled. "Who?"

"You." I tapped her on the nose.

"Really!" she exclaimed.

"Yep." I stepped behind the counter and pulled the bag from the shelf and handed it to Charley. "I bought these outfits for you a while ago. I was saving them for your birthday, but I think now is as good a time as any to give them to you."

She opened the bag and took out the articles of clothing with a big smile on her face. "Lily, I love them. Thank you," she said as she hugged me.

"Go in that room over there and get changed. I'll do your hair and then we'll have a photograph session. I think it would be a great gift for your mom and dad. Plus, you will look amazing hanging on my wall."

Charley went to change and I heard my phone ring. Maddie was calling.

"Hi, Maddie."

"Hi, Lily. I just wanted to let you know that my parents are having a birthday party for Charley this weekend at their house and I'm hoping you'll come. I know Charley would be devastated if you didn't and my parents would be upset as well. Luke told them what happened, but my mom said that you're still a part of the family and she wants you to come."

"I don't know, Maddie."

"Listen, I totally understand the awkwardness, but if for anything, do it for Charley. It's just one day. Plus, Adam and I want you there."

She was right. I had to think about Charley and nothing else. It was her birthday and the last thing I wanted to do was ruin it.

"I'll be there, Maddie."

"Great. Thank you, Lily. The party starts at noon and it's all day. I'll talk to you later."

Charley walked in with her first outfit on. She looked so cute.

"I love this outfit!" She smiled.

I walked over to her and ran my fingers through her hair. "I'm thinking maybe some curls would complete this adorable outfit."

We walked back to the changing room, where I had the makeup vanity set up. She sat in the black chair and we talked while I curled her hair.

"Someone has a birthday coming up." I smiled.

"I know. I can't wait." She giggled. "I thought this year's birthday was going to be the best ever because my dad is back. But now, you and Uncle Luke aren't talking to each other, so I guess it won't be so great after all."

I felt the biggest ache in my heart after hearing Charley say that. She didn't understand and it killed me to see her hurting so much.

"Charley, things are complicated right now between me and your Uncle Luke. I can't explain it to you because you're too young. But, I can promise you that you're going to have the best birthday ever! I'm going to make sure of it. I don't want you to worry about me and Luke anymore. In fact, I don't want you to be mad at him. He loves you more than life and it really hurt him deep down that you won't talk to him. This is a grown-up situation and there are no sides to be taken. Make sense?"

She nodded her head and then looked down. I lifted her chin as I swept a little bit of pink blush across her cheeks. I brought her curls over her shoulders and she smiled as she stared at herself in the mirror.

"Come on, Miss Model; let's get this photo shoot rolling."

She giggled as she got up from the chair and we headed to the photography room. After we had some dinner and ice cream, I walked Charley up to her apartment. As soon as we reached the top step, the door opened and Luke walked out.

"Hi, Uncle Luke." Charley smiled.

"Hey, peanut. How was your day?"

"It was great. Lily and I had so much fun!"

"That's great." He smiled as he patted her on the head and looked at me.

Maddie came to the door and thanked me. I said goodbye to Charley and then headed for the stairs.

"Hey, Lily?" Luke said as he followed me down the stairs. "About Charley's birthday. I don't want it to be awkward for either of us or her. I appreciate you putting everything that happened aside to come and be a part of her birthday."

"It's for Charley. I wouldn't hurt that little girl. I want her to have the best birthday ever, so let's make sure that she does."

He gave me a small smile as I went into my apartment and he went into his.

Chapter 22

Lily

"Great studio, Lily," Wyatt said as he walked around.

"Thank you. Let's go over tomorrow's shoot."

We spent the next two hours going over the location, equipment, and overall plan. Wyatt was great and I knew I had made the right decision hiring him.

"Lily, is that what I think it is?!" he asked in excitement as he stared at one of my cameras on the shelf.

"Yep. It sure is."

"Oh my God. I've always dreamed of shooting with this kind of camera."

"Go ahead and snap some pics. I don't mind." I smiled as I turned around and continued looking at some orders.

He took the camera outside and, when he walked in, he called my name. When I turned around, he snapped a picture of me.

"Are you done playing?" I asked.

"Yeah. Thanks. I need to go now. I have a class I need to get to. I'll meet you at the pier at eleven to set up."

Sandi Lynn

"Sounds great, Wyatt. Enjoy the rest of your day."

Later that evening, as I opened the building door, I saw Luke unlocking his door and Cody standing next to him. My stomach instantly felt sick and twisted and my heart started beating at a rapid pace. He looked at me.

"Oh, hey. Hi, Lily." Cody smiled.

"Hi," I softly said as I opened my door. Once I stepped inside and closed it, I leaned my back up against it and began to cry.

Did I have the right to cry? My chest felt heavy and my breathing felt constricted. I had wrapped myself in a cocoon to protect myself from feeling any more hurt. Obviously, my cocoon wasn't tight enough because the pain and hurt were seeping through at a rapid pace.

****

Luke

I gave Cody the files that I left on the counter and escorted her to the door. The look on Lily's face when she saw her standing there was torturous. I could only imagine what she thought. Fuck. Maybe I should have gone over and explained. She would probably have slapped me. I pulled my phone from my pocket and began to send her a text message. I stopped. She was the one who wouldn't give me the time of day and she probably wouldn't have believed me anyway. I set my phone on the counter and picked up my guitar. As I was strumming a tune, there was a knock at the door. I jumped up, hoping it was Lily. It wasn't.

"Lucky. Come on in."

149

"Hey, man. I need to talk to you for a minute."

"Sure. Beer?" I asked.

"Yeah."

"What's up? Is everything okay with Giselle and the baby?"

"Yeah, they're fine. I love her, bro. I mean, I'm in love with her."

I sat there confused. "Okay. Are we talking about Giselle?"

"Of course we're talking about Giselle. I want us to be a couple."

"As in marriage?"

"No. I'm not ready for marriage. I want us to be exclusive."

"You do know that means you can't be hitting on other women, right?"

"I know that. I don't want to see other women. I only want Giselle. Despite some of her annoying ways and flaws, I love her."

"That's great, bro. But your emotions are running really high right now. I think you should wait."

"That's what Sam said. Oh well. Maybe you're right. When are we going to play at the bar again? I'm missing it."

"Funny you should mention that. I was watching a band audition today and thinking the same thing."

"Then let's do it." He smiled. "I think all of us need to get back to some normalcy."

I chuckled. He was right and music was the perfect place to start.

"I'll look at my schedule and let you and Sam know. You're a daddy now and you're going to be busy."

"Nah, never too busy for the band. I'm off, bro. I need to get back to the hospital. Thanks for the talk."

When he left, I picked up my guitar again and started strumming the song "Don't Fear the Reaper" by Blue Oyster Cult. It was time to escape inside my music.

****

Lily

I opened up my laptop and connected the camera to it. I hadn't had the chance to go over all the pictures I took of Charley and I wanted them done in time for her birthday. When the file opened, I noticed the picture that Wyatt took of me. I was looking over my shoulder and the way he captured the look on my face was unnerving. I had a look of sadness, torture, and distress. Was that how people really saw me? I shook my head as I poured another glass of wine. I scrolled through the pictures of Charley and was very happy with the results. I picked my favorites and, as I began to edit them, I could hear Luke playing his guitar through the wall. I sipped my wine, edited my pictures, and took in the sound of the melody he played.

The next morning, I called Dr. Blakely to see if she had time to see me after my photo shoot. I had packed the Explorer yesterday with everything I needed from the studio, so I had some extra time this morning before I had to leave. I heard Luke's door shut and then there was knock on my door. I opened it and Luke was standing there, holding something in his hand.

"Sorry to bother you, but I have to change the furnace filter. It's that time of year. I figured I better do it now while you're home and before I head to the bar."

I waved my hand for him to come in, but didn't say a word. Looking at him made me crazy because all I could picture was Cody. I went to the kitchen to pour another cup of coffee and I heard Luke cuss from the hallway. I didn't react.

"Lily, can you grab me a towel? I'm bleeding."

Shit. I walked over and handed him the towel.

"Thanks," he said as he wrapped the side of his hand.

"Are you okay?"

"I'm fine," he said as he shut the door to the furnace.

I could see the blood soaking through the towel. "Luke, what did you do?"

"I cut myself on a piece of metal that I never shaved down like I was supposed to."

"Let me see," I said as I made him sit down at the table and I slowly removed the towel from his hand. "Oh God, you need stitches."

"I'm fine. I don't need anything. I have to go. If it doesn't stop soon, then I'll go to the ER."

"It's not going to stop. It's a deep gash." I looked at the clock. I had three hours before I had to be at the photo shoot. I grabbed another towel from the linen closet and replaced the blood-soaked one.

"Come on; I'm driving. Don't get blood on my seats," I said as I grabbed my keys.

"Lily, I'm fine."

"GET YOUR ASS IN THE TRUCK NOW!"

"Watch your mouth," he said with a slight smile.

We climbed in and I took off. "Keep it wrapped tight."

"I'm trying."

"They better not be busy because I have a photo shoot in less than three hours."

I pulled up to the doors of the ER and told him to go inside and that I'd meet him as soon as I parked. By time I found a spot, they had already put him in a room.

"Excuse me, but where is Luke Matthews?" I asked the nurse.

"Right this way," she said as she led me down the hall.

I walked in and Luke was sitting up with his hand over a silver tray.

"The doctor will be in shortly. Just hold on," the nurse said.

"You can go. I'll get a ride back," he said as he looked at me.

"Do you want me to call Cody for you?" Shit. The words just slipped out.

He looked down. "No, Lily, and what you saw yesterday was business. I left a folder on the counter that she needed and she followed me back to get it because I wasn't going back to the bar."

"You don't need to explain anything to me. It's none of my business."

"I didn't want you to think anything else," he said just as the doctor walked in.

He gave Luke a tetanus shot and then placed five stitches in the side of his hand.

"Okay, you're good to go. Keep that dry for the first twenty-four hours."

"Thanks, Doc."

He got up from the bed and looked at me. "Thank you, Lily. I appreciate it."

"You're welcome," I softly replied.

We climbed back into the Explorer and, on the way home, Luke asked me a question.

"Did you say you have a photo shoot today? That's great. I'm happy for you."

"Thanks. It's for *Prim* Magazine. It's their fall fashion shoot. We're doing it at the Santa Monica Pier."

Why the hell did I just tell him all that?

"Congratulations. You'll do great." He smiled.

His smile. It made me weak every time. It always did. Even in the middle of an argument, he would smile and I would instantly forget what we were arguing about.

"Thanks."

I dropped Luke off at the door and told him I had to get to the pier. He gave me a small wave before closing the car door.

Chapter 23

Luke

"What happened to you?" Maddie asked as I walked in the bar.

"I cut myself changing the furnace filter. There was a piece of metal I forgot to shave down."

"Ouch. Are you okay?"

"It hurts a little, but I'm fine."

"How did you drive to the hospital?"

"Lily drove me. It actually happened in her apartment while I was changing her filter. Oh, by the way, I'll be changing yours later tonight."

"Oh, okay. How did that go? I mean with Lily driving you to the hospital."

"It went okay. Is Cody here?"

"Yeah, she's in your office."

"I have a few errands to run. I need to go get Charley's birthday present and some flowers for Mom. I'll be back later."

I hopped into the Jeep and drove to the guitar store, where I picked out a nice guitar that Charley could grow with. I then headed to the flower shop down the road and I bought two dozen roses. One dozen was for my mom and the other was for Lily. I wanted to thank her for taking me to the hospital, but I was not so sure they'd be well received. It was a small gesture. A thank you. How could she deny that? She still cared about me, even though when I looked at her, all I saw was anger in her eyes. Maybe tomorrow, at Charley's party, we could make a little bit of progress. I liked to think that was what happened today when she drove me to the hospital. Progress. One day at a time. I'd get her back and our love would be stronger than it was before.

****

Lily

It was a perfect day for the photo shoot. It went better than I expected, thanks to Wyatt and his assistance. The day seemed to fly by. Since it was my first magazine photo shoot, I was in my glory and I loved every minute of it. When we wrapped, Adalynn asked if we could finish up the shoot on Monday morning at the studio. She overbooked a couple of the models and they needed to be somewhere else. I told her that it was fine and I'd be there. As Wyatt and I were gathering the equipment, I looked over and saw the Ferris wheel that Luke and I went on together when we first brought Charley here. I remembered being so scared because I hated heights, but he made me face my fear, and when I did, I saw things differently. I'd never forget that night.

"Hey, are you okay?" Wyatt asked.

"Yeah. I'm fine," I said as I snapped back into reality.

We loaded the equipment in the back of the Explorer and I hugged Wyatt goodbye.

"You are an amazing assistant and I want to keep you working for me. I really don't have much for you to do right now, but I'll be in touch."

"Sounds great, Lily. I had a great time. Let's do coffee, lunch, or dinner."

"Definitely!" I smiled as I climbed into the Explorer and drove to Dr. Blakely's office.

"Come on in, Lily." She smiled as she opened her office door. "Tell me what you've been doing since our last session."

I sat down in the oversized leather chair and brought my knees up to my chest.

"I went back to Seattle and confronted Brynn and Hunter."

"Oh? How did that go?"

"It went better than I expected. I didn't break down or murder them like I thought I might. They explained that they didn't do it to hurt me and that it was something that just happened. They tried to stop it but couldn't because they loved each other. I finally realized that I was the middleman in bringing them together."

"How do you feel about that?"

"It still hurts and I don't think our relationship will ever go back to what it was. But, I can understand that when two people are supposed to be together in this life, nothing can tear them apart."

"Like you and Luke?" she asked.

I wrapped my arms around my legs and looked at her.

"By the way you're sitting, it seems like you're protecting yourself from something."

"Maybe I am."

"Tell me about Luke."

"He wants to talk and explain himself. He said he was sorry and he didn't mean it. I won't let him in. I don't want to hear what he has to say."

"Why is that?" she asked.

"Because I'm angry. So angry."

"Angry at what? What are you really angry about, Lily? The fact that he accused you of Callie's death or the fact that he left you because of her?"

I looked at her blankly and then lowered my head to my knees.

"Lily? Am I right? Your father left you, so to speak, when he cheated on your mother. He left you physically and emotionally. Hunter left you when he cheated on you with Brynn. Now, Luke left you when he found out you were the one that gave him the tickets. His reason was because of Callie. It's always been in the back of your mind that he still cared for her more than you and that him leaving because of something that involved her confirmed it for you that night."

I lifted my head and looked across the room. "Everyone that has been a vital part of my life has left me. My father, my biological mother, my fiancé, Luke. When he walked out that door and left me standing there, I felt like I had been prosecuted and he was the attorney that closed the case and walked out of the courtroom," I said as the tears began to fall from my eyes. "He said that Callie would still be alive today if I hadn't given them the tickets. At first, I was so scared that he would never forgive me and that he'd hate me. But then anger started to settle inside me."

She handed me a tissue. "It sounds to me like he realized what he did and how badly he hurt you. He wants to apologize and you won't let him. Why is that? Do you want to hurt him like he hurt you? An eye for an eye? Or are you just protecting yourself from ever being hurt again? Because if you forgive him, then that would mean you run the risk of him hurting you or of you hurting him."

"Luke has already been hurt enough by me. I've caused him so much pain and heartache. If I let him back into my life, he'll hurt more. Every time he looks at me, he'll be reminded of how I was the one; that girl that caused Callie's death. I love him too much to watch him go through that. So it's best that I stay away."

"And there it is." She smiled as she reached over and took hold of my hand. "You aren't angry at Luke; you're angry at yourself."

I nodded. She was right.

"So you're letting him go so you don't cause him any more pain?"

I nodded again.

"Don't you think that you should let Luke decide that? Are you being fair to him by letting him suffer two losses?"

"Two?" I asked.

"Yes. The loss of Callie and now you."

"He'll be fine eventually. He doesn't need to be reminded of what happened when he looks at me."

"Do you honestly think that's how he feels?"

"I think so."

"Well, I think you're mistaken and you need to talk to him."

I got up from my seat when I noticed that we were thirty minutes over our allotted session time.

"Thank you for seeing me, Dr. Blakely. I'll give everything you've said consideration."

****

Luke

Before I headed back to the bar, I set the bouquet of roses outside of Lily's door. When I walked into my apartment, Gretchen was getting ready to leave.

"Hey, Luke. You shouldn't have." She smiled.

"Sorry, Gretchen. They're for my mom."

"What did you do to your hand?"

"I cut it over at Lily's place while I was changing the furnace filter. It hurts like a bitch."

"Stiches?"

"Yep, five."

"Ouch. Feel better. I have to run. I have my first photo shoot since the accident." She smiled.

"Congratulations. I'll see you later."

I walked in the kitchen and pulled out a vase from the cupboard. I set the roses for my mom in some water to keep them fresh for tomorrow. I heard the door open and Gretchen walked back in.

"Hey, you didn't by any chance leave some roses for Lily, did you?"

"Yeah. Those are from me. She drove me to the hospital and I wanted to thank her."

"Aw, she'll love them."

"Or hate them and me for giving them to her."

"Stop being negative. She'll come around. Time, Luke. Remember that."

I sighed because that was what everyone kept telling me. I hated time. I hated waiting. I craved her arms wrapped around me. I longed to hold her and to tell her how much I loved her.

Chapter 24

Lily

I stopped by the studio to drop off the majority of the equipment before I headed home. When I opened the door to the building, I saw a bouquet of roses sitting outside my door, wrapped in a pretty pink print paper. Attached was a card. As I picked up the roses and unlocked the door, I set my keys down and walked over to the table, where I pulled the card out and opened it.

"Lily, thank you for taking me to the hospital this morning.

I appreciate it.

Love,

Luke"

I picked up the roses and smelled them. The fragrance was calming as I lightly touched the smooth petal that curled up with my finger, taking in their silky nap. They were beautiful, just like our relationship used to be. I took a vase from the cabinet and filled it with water, arranging the roses inside, one by one. I set the vase in the middle of the kitchen table and softly smiled as they brightened up my apartment, which had been nothing but dark and dreary lately. I needed to thank Luke for the flowers because I wasn't the cold, heartless bitch that everyone seemed to think I was. I was protecting the one I loved. If you love someone, you'll set them free. Isn't that how it goes? I picked up my phone and sent him a text message.

"You're welcome and thank you for the beautiful roses. You shouldn't have done that. It was unnecessary."

"You're welcome and it was necessary. I hope you'll keep them."

I tapped the camera button on my phone and snapped a picture of the roses in the vase and then sent it to Luke.

"They look great on the table."

"They certainly do," he replied.

****

I didn't roll out of bed until after nine a.m., when I was awakened by another nightmare, covered in sweat with my heart beating rapidly. Today was Charley's birthday and party, and I needed to get ready to drive out to Luke's parents' house. I didn't know what this day was going to bring emotion-wise, but I had to keep positive and happy for Charley. As soon as I stepped out of the shower, I heard my phone ringing. I grabbed it from the nightstand in my bedroom and saw that Luke's mom was calling. My stomach did a sick flip.

"Hello," I answered nervously.

"Hi, sweetheart. It's Annie."

"Hi, Annie. How are you?"

"I'm doing okay. Listen, the reason why I'm calling is because I want to tell you how happy Tom and I are that you're coming to Charley's party today."

"I wouldn't miss it for the world."

"I wanted to make it very clear that no matter what's going on between you and Luke, it doesn't affect how we feel about you. We don't want you to feel out of place or awkward in our home. You're just as welcome and loved here as anyone else."

Hearing her say those words to me was comforting. I was nervous about seeing them and not knowing how they felt about the situation.

"Thank you, Annie. That really means a lot."

"You're welcome, sweetheart. We'll see you later. Bye."

"Bye." I hung up and felt a little more at ease.

****

I pulled up into the driveway of Tom and Annie's house and grabbed the bottle of wine that I had stopped and picked up on the way. Before getting out of the Explorer, I took in a deep breath and tried to calm my knotted, sick-feeling stomach. This wasn't going to be easy. I walked up to the door with perfect composure and lightly knocked. After a few moments, Annie opened the door and hugged me.

"Thank you for coming, Lily."

"This is for you." I smiled as I handed her the wine.

"Oh, you're such a doll. Thank you."

"Hi, Lily." Adam smiled as he walked over and lightly hugged me.

"LILY!" Charley exclaimed as she came running from the kitchen and threw her arms around me.

"Happy birthday, Charley." I smiled as I picked her up and kissed the tip of her nose.

I put her down and she took my hand and led me to the kitchen, which was decorated with birthday signs and balloons.

"Lily, it's so good to see you." Tom smiled as he hugged me.

"It's good to see you too, Tom."

Luke was bent over in the refrigerator and turned around and looked at me. He gave me a small smile, twisted the cap off his beer, and then went outside to the patio. Not too long after, Gretchen and Sam showed up.

"How did the photo shoot go?" she asked.

"It was amazing. I loved every minute of it."

"Hey, Lily," Sam said as he walked over and kissed my head. "You okay?"

"Yeah." I smiled with uncertainty.

I asked Maddie if she could come into the kitchen and I handed her the box that contained the photos of Charley.

"Here; these are for you."

She smiled as she carefully took off the lid and gasped when she saw the pictures of Charley.

"Lily, these are beautiful. Oh my God. Look at our little girl, Adam."

"Wow, Lily." He smiled as he looked at them.

Sandi Lynn

Luke walked in from the patio and came over to see what we were all looking at.

"Lily, those are wonderful pictures. Look at how cute Charley is."

"Thanks," I said. "How's your hand?"

"It's so-so. It still hurts a little." He smiled as he put his hand on the small of my back and walked away. I froze. It was only for a mere second, but it felt like his touch was imprinted into my skin. I sat down on the patio next to Gretchen while Maddie, Sam, and Luke helped the kids with the party games. I couldn't stop staring at him and the way he was with the kids.

"You okay?" Gretchen asked.

"Yeah, why?"

"Because you seem to be in a daze and staring at Luke. I know how much you love him, so why are you fighting it? Just work things out with the man. How long are you going to let this go?"

"It's complicated, Gretchen. You don't understand."

"What's complicated about two people who are deeply and madly in love working things out? Luke wants you back. He told me so."

"He thinks he wants me back," I said with a tear in my eye.

"What do you mean by that, Lily?"

I got up from my chair and looked down at her. "It means exactly how it sounds. Now if you'll excuse me, I need to get another drink."

I walked into the house. Annie was getting Charley's birthday cake ready.

"Is there anything I can do to help, Annie?"

"No, sweetheart. Just sit back and enjoy yourself." She smiled.

Enjoy myself. How the hell was I supposed to enjoy myself when I was nothing but miserable. It took everything I had to come and be with Luke's family. The party was a huge success and Charley was happy. That was all that mattered. I took my margarita that Tom had made for me and stepped back out onto the patio. The only seat available was one next to Luke. I took in a deep breath and sat down.

"Hey."

"Hey," I replied.

"The party was a success and Charley seemed to have a great time," he said.

"It was a great party."

As we sat there in awkward silence, Luke reached over and touched my hair. I looked at him and he smiled.

"Sorry. You had a small leaf in your hair."

"Thanks," I said as I ran my hand through my hair.

Now when I looked at him, the only thing that my mind would think was how much he resented me for everything that happened. He only thought he wanted us back together, until he realized that he couldn't be around me every day and night because I would be the constant reminder of what happened to

Callie. Just like I was the constant reminder to my mother about my father's affair.

Chapter 25

Luke

It had been a week since Charley's party and I hadn't seen Lily. But then again, I hadn't been coming home from the bar until the middle of the night. Lucky and Giselle were bringing the baby home next week, so Sam and I decided to get the nursery ready for them. Gretchen wanted to help, but she had to go out of town for a photo shoot. Lucky wasn't very handy, and we didn't trust him with paint and putting together the furniture. It was a Saturday afternoon and we were going to start painting. Giselle had all the colors picked out before she went into labor and had the paint delivered. So all we needed to do was get it up on the walls. We had just arrived and were laying down the plastic on the floor when we heard someone walk through the door.

"What are you two doing here?" Lily asked.

"Painting," Sam replied. "What are you doing here?"

"I picked up some things for the baby, so I thought I'd drop them off. Plus, I was going to clean up around here. I didn't know anyone else would be here."

"Surprise," I said.

She walked away and Sam's phone beeped.

"Ah, shit. I gotta go, bro. Work needs me. Apparently, there's a big problem with one of the accounts."

"What?! It's Saturday, man."

"I know. Sorry. I'll try to get it worked out and come back," he said as he walked out the door.

I shook my head as I poured some paint in the paint tray and Lily walked in.

"Where did Sam go?"

"Work. Something happened with one of his accounts."

"Oh."

I rolled the paint on the wall and Lily stood there, staring at me.

"Is something wrong?" I asked.

"Since Sam had to leave, I can help you paint if you want."

"Nah. I'm fine."

"I can paint, you know."

"I never said you couldn't."

"You refusing my help tells me that you think I can't paint a wall."

"Where are you getting that from? That's not what I'm saying."

"Good. Then I can help."

I sighed. "There's an extra roller over there. Be my guest."

I found myself having a little bit of an attitude with her because being in the same room with her, especially after not seeing her for a week, killed me. We still never talked about that night. She wouldn't. I didn't know what to do anymore to try and get her to listen to me. Sometimes, I felt like I just needed to give up, but the thought destroyed me.

****

Lily

He was Mr. Attitude today. Was I surprised? No. I hadn't seen him for a week and it was the one of the longest weeks of my life. But then again, I wasn't home much. I spent my days and most nights at the studio, editing the pictures from the photo shoot for *Prim*. I had delivered the photos to Adalynn and she loved them and immediately booked my services for another shoot next month. Things in my career zone seemed to be moving forward, but my personal life stayed at a miserable standstill. Silence filled the room. The only significant sound that was heard was the sticky noise of the paint being rolled on the walls.

"Are you going to be able to paint with your hand like that?" I asked.

"I'll be fine."

Luke put down his paint roller and turned on the radio. The song that was on was ending and "Don't Fear the Reaper" began to play. That was the tune I heard Luke playing on his guitar that one night.

"This was one of Dad's favorite songs. He used to sing and play it all the time. I always wondered about the meaning behind it."

"It's about eternal love," Luke said.

"Oh. Then, clearly, my father wasn't thinking about my mother when he would sing it."

Luke laughed. "Lily!"

"What?" I smiled as I turned around and looked at him.

He stared at me for a moment, looking for something to say. "I'm hungry. Are you?" he asked.

"A little."

"How about we order some pizza and take a break. The first coat is going to have to dry before we can put on the second coat anyway."

"Pizza sounds good." I smiled.

"The usual?" he asked as he pulled out his phone.

"Yeah. The usual."

For the first time since that life-altering night, my stomach wasn't twisted in a knot. It felt somewhat normal and I didn't know what to think. As Luke called in our pizza order, my phone beeped with a text message from Sam.

"Is Luke pissed that I'm not there?"

"No. I'm helping him paint the room."

"Oh. Thank you. I appreciate it. Unfortunately, I have to go out of town for a couple of days to smooth things over with this account, so I'll see you when I get back."

"Have fun!"

"You too!"

"The pizza will be here in about twenty minutes," Luke said.

"I just got a text message from Sam and he said he has to go out of town for a couple of days for work."

"Is that so?" He sighed.

I walked to the kitchen and washed off the spots of paint that were all over my hands. I took two paper plates from the cupboard and set them on the table. Luke walked in and went straight to the refrigerator.

"Beer?" he asked as he held up a bottle.

"Sure," I said as I walked over and took it from him.

Luke took a seat at the table while I put the bags that I'd brought over on the couch.

"What did you buy?"

"Just some baby stuff. Towels, wash cloths, burp rags, bibs. You know, the usual baby things."

"I still can't believe the two of them had a baby," Luke smirked.

I shook my head as I took the seat across from him. "I know. I sure hope they can stand each other long enough for that little girl."

Luke threw his head back and laughed. "I was thinking the same thing."

I smiled as I arched my eyebrow and held up my beer bottle. A few moments later, there was a knock at the door. I went in my purse and took some cash out and handed it to Luke.

"No, Lily. It's on me."

"No. Take it."

He opened the door and it was Gary, our normal pizza delivery guy from the apartment.

"Hey, you two. Did you move?"

"Hey, Gary." Luke smiled. "Nah, this is our friend's house. We're doing some work."

I tried to hand Luke the money and he kept shooing my hand away. Gary looked at me and smiled.

"Lily, Luke always pays. What are you doing?"

"Exactly!" Luke smirked.

I sighed and took the pizza over to the table. Later, I would shove the money in the pocket of the hoodie he brought. We sat down and each took a couple of slices. It felt normal. Like the way things used to be.

"How's your mom doing?" he asked out of the clear blue.

I took a sip of my beer before answering him. "She's good. Why?"

Luke shrugged his shoulders. "I heard you tell Charley that you went back to Seattle. How did that go? You know with—"

"Brynn?" I interrupted.

"Yeah."

"We talked and we cried. Same with Hunter, without the crying part."

"You saw him?"

"Yeah. They're still together and oh so in love. It made me realize a few things and see things in a different light."

Instantly, I saw a change in his face. "So let me get this straight. You went all the way to Seattle to talk to your sister and ex-fiancé about their relationship and what they did to you, but you refuse to talk to me about us? That's real nice, Lily," he said as he got up from his chair, threw the plate in the garbage, and then walked out of the kitchen.

Great. Just fucking great. I didn't know what to do. I cleaned up the table and put the leftover pizza in the refrigerator. When I walked back into the room, Luke turned around and looked at me.

"You can leave now. I got this."

"Luke, please."

"Lily, I mean it. Get the hell out of here, NOW!" he yelled.

I flinched at the anger in his voice. Reaching into my pocket, I grabbed some cash and threw it on the floor.

"Fuck you, Luke. Just fuck you!" I yelled as I stormed out.

Chapter 26

Luke

I called Maddie and asked her if she could swing by Giselle's place. I needed to talk to someone, because if I didn't, I was going to lose it. It didn't take her long to come over because she was shopping in the area. When she walked in, she came right into the bedroom and grabbed a paint roller.

"What happened?"

"Lily. That's what happened. I just don't get it, sis. She goes back to Seattle and makes amends with her sister and that scumbag ex-fiancé of hers and it's okay, but she won't fucking talk to *me*. She won't talk about our relationship."

"Luke, you need to calm down for a minute."

"I told her to get the hell out of here, Maddie. I was so angry that she wouldn't talk to me."

She walked over to where I was standing and wrapped her arms around me. "There's something else going on."

"What do you mean?" I asked as I pulled back.

"I'm not so sure anymore that it's about the things you said to her. Your love for each other is so strong and so pure that it should be able to overcome anything. I don't know, Luke.

Maybe I'm crazy, but there's something else going on with Lily."

"Whatever the hell her problem is, I don't have time to waste anymore. I'm done and I mean it this time. If Lily doesn't want to talk to me or discuss what happened, then fine. She can go off and live a happy life by herself because, obviously, it's what she wants."

Maddie and I didn't say another word after that. She stayed and helped me finish the walls and then we headed home. Lily's truck wasn't in the parking lot and it was almost midnight. Not that I should have cared, but it wasn't safe. I said goodbye to Maddie and I stepped inside my apartment. Sam and Gretchen were both gone and I was all alone. There was no way I was going to sleep until I knew that Lily was home safe. About an hour later, as I was sitting on the couch, I heard her door shut.

****

The next morning, I went back over to Giselle's and helped Lucky build the crib. When I got there, he was sitting in the middle of the nursery, swearing up a storm with crib pieces and parts all over the floor.

"Dude, it's about time. Do you have any idea how fucked up this is?"

I chuckled. "They aren't that hard to build. Move over and hand me the directions."

"How's Lily?"

"Why are you asking me?"

"Sam said she was over here yesterday, helping you paint. Oh, by the way, thanks for doing that."

"Things were going good until she told me something and I told her to get the hell out," I replied.

"Whoa, dude. Come on. What the fuck is going on?"

"She went to Seattle to talk to her sister and ex and she won't talk to me," I said as I grabbed the screwdriver.

"She talks to you. I've seen her."

"She won't talk about us. She can forgive and talk to the people who cheated on her and made her life a living hell, but she can't talk to me about our relationship."

"Well, you did tell her that she killed Callie."

"Thanks for that, Lucky. I don't want to talk about Lily anymore."

Just as I was tightening one of the bolts, my phone rang. It was Cody.

"Hey, Cody. What's up?"

"Hi, Luke. Sorry to bother you on a Sunday, but I think there's a problem with the invoice for the liquor order."

"It's your day off. Why are you at the bar?"

"I had nothing else to do today, so I thought I'd come in. Do you think you can stop by later and have a look?"

"Yeah. I'm in the middle of building the crib for Giselle and Lucky's baby. I'll be there in a while."

"Thanks. I'll be waiting."

I hung up and looked over at Lucky, who was staring at me. "Dude, she is so into you. You better be careful."

"She is not," I snapped.

"Yes, she is. I know when women are into guys. I know their tricks and, trust me, she's into you."

An hour later, the crib was built and put in its place and, after I helped Lucky clean up, I took off for the bar.

When I arrived, I walked straight to my office and saw Cody sitting behind my desk. She was holding the picture that I had in my drawer of me and Lily.

"What are you doing?" I asked.

"Oh, Luke. Sorry. I was just looking at your picture."

"Why?"

"I couldn't find a paperclip, so I opened the drawer and there it was. I'm sorry."

I walked over and took it from her hands.

"It's a nice picture."

"I'm not here to talk about the picture. What's up with the invoice?" I asked.

"I'm sorry. I already figured it out. I forgot to call you. But since you're here, would you like to go grab a bite to eat?"

"No. I already ate. Since the invoice is fine, you can go now."

"Okay," she said with a sad look as she grabbed her purse and started to walk out the door. She turned around. "You're a really nice and special guy. You shouldn't be alone. If you would like some company, call me."

I nodded. Maybe Lucky was right. I was going to have to keep a closer eye on her. After talking to Candi for a bit, I decided to go home. I couldn't stop thinking about Lily and how rude I was to her last night. I needed to apologize. When I pulled in the parking lot, her Explorer was in its usual spot. I knocked on her door before going to my apartment.

"Luke," she said as she opened the door.

"I need to talk to you."

"I think you said enough last night," she said.

"Please, Lily. I want to apologize for my behavior last night. I was way out of line and I'm sorry."

She motioned for me to come inside.

"I just want you to know that I'm not going to try and push you to talk to me anymore. What's done is done and obviously, I can't change that night. I didn't mean what I said and you are in no way responsible for what happened. I was a jerk and I was in shock. That's all. I would give anything to rewind that night and do things right. I'm really happy that you talked to Hunter and Brynn because I know it had been weighing heavy on your mind for a long time."

She stood across the room and listened to every word I said. She never interrupted and she never moved from her spot.

"I just wanted you to know that. I'll leave you to whatever it was you were doing." As soon as I put my hand on the doorknob, she spoke.

"Thank you, Luke. I appreciate you saying what you did."

I nodded and gave her a small smile as I walked out the door.

Chapter 27

Lily

He was hurting; I could tell. He was hurting just as bad as I was. This pain he was feeling would pass. The pain of looking at me, talking to me, and making love to me would always be there in the back of his mind if we were together. Maybe he wouldn't realize it at first, but little things would remind him of Callie and then he'd look at me, wishing that I'd never given him those tickets. It wasn't only about how he felt; it was also about the guilt that I would carry for the rest of my life. Maybe I was protecting the both of us.

I spent the next week photographing children and helping Gretchen plan Giselle's baby shower that was going to be held at Luke's bar. He offered and Gretchen jumped on it without talking to me first. She thought it would be perfect and so did Giselle. Since the shower was today and I hadn't seen or talked to Luke since that Sunday he stopped by, it was going to be awkward. As I was putting the shower favors that I was in charge of in the box, there was a knock at the door.

"Come on in. It's open," I yelled.

The door opened and I heard Luke's voice from behind.

"Hey, Lily."

After I gasped, I turned around. "Hi, Luke."

"I was wondering if you needed any help with the boxes for the shower. Gretchen said that you'd have a few. I could load them in the jeep."

He looked so hot. As I stared at him, my mind went to all the times we made love. I missed him so much that I didn't know what to do anymore. Gretchen and Giselle told me every day how stupid I was, but they didn't know the real reason I couldn't let him back into my life.

"I have these right here," I said as I pointed to the boxes on the table.

"Are they ready to go?"

"Yeah."

He walked over to the table and grabbed the first box and then looked at me and smiled.

"You look beautiful."

I could feel myself blushing as I thanked him. He gave me a small smile as he loaded the boxes in his jeep.

"Okay, I guess that's it. I'll see you at the bar."

The bar was decorated throughout with pink balloons and streamers. When I walked in, the first person I saw was Cody. *What the hell is she doing here?* Sam walked over to me and kissed me on the cheek.

"You look gorgeous, Lily."

"Thanks, Sam."

"I live right next door to you and I haven't seen you lately."

"I've been busy at the studio and then, with planning the shower, I really haven't had much time for anything else."

"Well, stop being a stranger; I miss you." He smiled.

"I miss you too," I said as I patted his chest.

The shower got underway and was a huge success. A little over a hundred people came and showered Giselle and Lucky with gifts for Isabella. Luke was behind the bar making drinks when I walked up.

"Hi. What can I get you?" he asked.

"A glass of red wine will be fine."

He smiled and, as he was pouring it into a glass, Adalynn walked up to me.

"Lily, I need to talk to you about something."

"Sure, Adalynn. What's up?"

"How would you like to go to New York for a couple of weeks?"

"That would be great. What's happening in New York?"

"I'm launching a fashion blog and I would like you to do the fashion shoot for it."

"I would love to."

"Great. I know it's kind of last minute, but I need you to leave the day after tomorrow. It's a two-week shoot and *Prim* will pay all your expenses. I knew you'd be game, so I booked you a room at The Trump. It overlooks Central Park and that's where I want the majority of the shoot."

I could feel Luke's eyes on me as Adalynn and I were talking. As soon as she walked away, he spoke up.

"Wow. New York. That's exciting," he said.

Suddenly, Cody stepped behind the bar and put her arm around his waist. "When you get a chance, I need to talk to you in private."

"Excuse me, Lily," he said as he walked away with her.

My stomach started to flip out and I became overly hot. Was he seeing her? Was that why he came over and told me that he wasn't going to pressure me into talking to him anymore? Thoughts of the two of them together consumed me and I felt like I couldn't breathe. I walked towards the back to see if I could hear their conversation and when I approached Luke's office, I saw him kiss her on her forehead as he clasped her shoulders. I put my hand over my mouth and quietly walked away so he didn't hear me. I went into the main area of the bar and found Adalynn.

"If it's okay with you, I'm going to leave tonight for New York. I haven't been there since I was a kid and I think I should scout out locations in Central Park first."

"Great idea! I didn't think of that. I'll call the hotel and tell them you'll be arriving tonight and you can fly on the company jet. Give me a second and let me check the flight schedules."

As she pulled out her phone, I looked over and saw Luke and Cody. He had his hand on the small of her back as they walked into the main area.

"Great news. Your flight leaves at seven o'clock." She smiled.

I looked at my watch and saw it was four. I guessed I had better get home and get packed.

"You're leaving tonight?" Luke said.

He must have overheard our conversation.

"Yeah," I replied as I turned around and began to walk away.

"I thought you weren't leaving for a couple of days."

"Change in plans. I need to get the fuck away from here." I didn't mean for those last few words to spew out of my mouth, but they did.

"Why the sudden change, Lily?"

"It's none of your business, Luke. Why don't you focus on your little girlfriend over there and leave me the hell alone."

By this time, all the guests had pretty much left. I told Giselle and Gretchen what was happening and that I had to leave and go pack. I hugged them goodbye and when I walked out of the bar, Luke was standing up against the Explorer.

"Get out of my way, Luke," I said.

"I'm not moving until you tell me what the hell that remark was about Cody."

"I saw you kiss her, Luke. Okay. There. You wanted to know, so I told you."

"When?" he asked in confusion.

"In your office. Just a little while ago."

He threw his head back and laughed. "Lily, she quit. I was wishing her good luck."

"Luke, I have to go. I have a lot of packing to do and a plane to catch, so if you'll excuse me and please move away from my vehicle, I'd appreciate it."

"Whatever, Lily. I'm over you." He hit the hood of the Explorer and walked away.

His words hurt, but what did I expect? Tears filled my eyes, as I would never get over him.

****

Luke

This was tearing me apart. I told her that I was over her and I wasn't. I'd never be. I was so in love with her that I had to put an end to all of this once and for all. We needed to talk and if I had to lock her in a room until I got some answers, I would. I called Candi over to join me behind the bar so I could talk to her and Maddie.

"What's up, boss?" she asked.

"I need the two of you to do me a favor. I need you to run the bar while I'm gone."

"Where are you going?" Maddie asked.

"I'm going to New York to get my girlfriend back. I'm done with this game and she's going to listen to me."

"Good for you, Luke." Candi smiled as she patted me on the back.

"What if she won't?" Maddie said.

"It's not even an option for her anymore. I'm going to ask Mom and Dad to help out here too. As you know, Cody quit."

"It's about time," Candi said.

"I had to have a little talk with her and she didn't like what I had to say, so she thought it would be best to move on."

"Smart girl." Maddie smiled. "When are you leaving?"

"I'm going to try and get a flight out of here first thing tomorrow morning."

Maddie and Candi both hugged me. "Good luck. You do whatever you have to and get her back."

"Trust me; I will."

I left the bar and called my parents. They said that they would be more than happy to help out at the bar while I was gone and my dad said not to worry about the paperwork or the books. As I was unlocking the door to my apartment, Lily walked out with two suitcases. She looked startled when she saw me.

"Let me help you with those," I said.

"No need. I've got this."

"Too fucking bad, Lily; I'm helping you," I said as I grabbed one of her suitcases from her hand.

"Watch your mouth, Matthews."

I silently smiled. I loaded her suitcase in the limo that Adalynn had sent over to pick her up. She climbed in and I stopped her from shutting the door. I poked my head inside.

"Have a good time in New York."

"Thank you," she said quietly.

Little did she know that she'd be seeing me tomorrow.

Chapter 28

Lily

I lay down on the plush king-size bed in the hotel room and took note of the bottle of champagne and plate of chocolate-covered strawberries sitting on the table in front of the window. I got up and walked over to find a card with my name on it.

"Enjoy your stay and have a great photo shoot.

Best, Ian and Adalynn, Prim *Magazine"*

I smiled as I set the card down and bit into a large, juicy strawberry. I had wished that Wyatt could have made the trip with me. But with his classes, he couldn't. I didn't know what I was going to do because I needed an assistant. I'd have to contact Adalynn and see if there was anyone here that would be willing to help. I walked into the bathroom and looked at the amazing sunken jet tub and decided it was time for a glass of champagne and a relaxing bubble bath. I started the water and got undressed. It was one in the morning here and I was still on California time.

As I poured myself a glass of champagne, I climbed into the bubbly tub and sank until the water reached my neck. I took a sip of my champagne and closed my eyes. I couldn't stop thinking about Luke and his attitude before I left for New York. The way he grabbed my suitcase from me was a bit rough.

Then the way he told me to have a good time in New York was weird. It sounded like he was happy that I was leaving. I didn't know. I couldn't put my finger on it, but he sounded different. Somewhere in the back of my mind, I had wished he was here with me. Exploring New York with him would have been fun under different circumstances. Once I was finished with my bath, I changed into my pajamas and climbed into bed. I was surprised at how quickly I fell asleep.

****

Luke

I checked into The Trump at ten a.m. Thank God my room was ready.

"Here you go, Mr. Matthews. You will be staying in room 2212. I'll have the bellhop bring up your luggage."

"Nah, that's okay. I can take it up myself. Thank you."

I boarded the elevator and rode it up to the twenty-second floor. This had to be the most beautiful place I'd ever stayed at. I was on the lookout for Lily but I hadn't planned out what I was going to say to her when I saw her. I had a feeling once she saw me, she'd be pissed. I sent a text message to Gretchen, asking her if she knew which room Lily was in.

"Do you know what room number Lily is in?"

"No. Hold on a sec and I'll see if Giselle knows."

I waited and, after a few moments, a text message came through.

"She doesn't know either. Sorry, Luke."

"It's okay. I'll think of something."

I left the hotel and walked a couple of blocks. It was going to be tough trying to find Lily here. It would be like trying to find a needle in a haystack. After a couple of hours and a Starbucks later, I pulled out my phone to see if I had any messages. As I was walking, I accidentally ran into someone, which wasn't hard to do in this city.

"I'm sor—" We both started to say at the same time as I looked up.

"LUKE! What the—"

"Lily. What a coincidence." I smiled with relief.

"What are you doing here?" she asked through gritted teeth.

"Can we go somewhere else and talk so we're not in the way of people?"

She grabbed me by the arm and pulled me over to the side. "Again. What are you doing here?"

"I came to talk to you."

"You flew all the way to New York to talk to me?"

"Yes, and you're going to damn well listen to me too!"

"Not right now I'm not. I have something to do," she snapped.

"Whatever it is you're doing, I'm doing it with you. You shouldn't be walking around this city by yourself."

She looked at me as she cocked her head. "It's my life and I'll do what I want. You are not my keeper and you cannot tell me what to do. Who the hell do you think you are, Luke Matthews?"

"I'm the guy who's in love with you and needs you to listen; that's who I am."

Her sad but angry eyes stared into mine for a moment and then she looked away. "I am not talking about this here, and I'm not talking about this now."

She turned around and started to walk away. I followed behind.

****

Lily

I couldn't believe Luke was here in New York City. I was so pissed off at him, but then again, I wasn't, if that made any sense. I reached the Trump and he followed me inside.

"Why are you following me? I'm going to my room and you're not coming."

"It just so happens that I'm going to my room too."

I stopped in the middle of the lobby. "You're staying here?" I asked.

"Yes." He smiled.

"Do you realize how expensive this place is?"

"Yes."

"You can't afford that."

"You don't worry about what I can and can't afford." He smiled.

"Go home, Luke," I said as I stepped onto the elevator.

"Nah, I think I'll stay in New York for a while."

I pushed the button to my floor and asked Luke which floor he was on.

"Same," he replied.

"You're on floor twenty-two?"

"Yep. I sure am."

When the elevator doors opened, I stepped out and walked to my room. I looked over at Luke, who stopped at the door next to mine.

"No. No. No. That is not your room!"

He smiled as he inserted the card into the lock and opened the door. "Is this a coincidence or maybe something else?"

"FUCK!"

"Watch your mouth, babe." He winked and then walked inside his room, shutting the door behind him.

I can't believe this, I thought as I walked into the room. I threw my purse on the bed and paced the floor before grabbing a chocolate-covered strawberry and shoving it into my mouth. I grabbed my phone from my purse and called Dr. Blakely.

"Dr. Blakely's office. How can I help you?"

"Regina, it's Lily Gilmore. I need to speak to Dr. Blakely."

"Would you like to make an appointment?"

"I can't since I'm in New York. But, if she has a moment, I need to speak to her."

"She's in with a patient right now. I'll give her your message."

"Thank you, Regina. Please tell her that it's very important."

I sat down on the bed, tapping my foot on the floor. "Call, call, call," I said as I stared at my phone. Why was this so hard? Why couldn't I make my own decision? Wait. I did. I made the decision to cease and desist. Okay, not in the form of a letter, but verbally. Why did his coming here have the profound effect of a smidge of happiness on me? Why did I suddenly feel comfort knowing that he was right next door? It was like we were back in California. My phone rang.

"Dr. Blakely, thank God you called."

"Lily, what's wrong? My secretary said you were in New York."

"I had to go to New York for work. Luke flew in this morning. He said he wanted to talk."

"He flew all the way to New York to talk to you?"

"Yes. What do I do? My head tells me to talk to him, but my heart is shaking in the corner and telling me no."

"First of all, you need to calm down and take in a deep, cleansing breath. It's inevitable, Lily, that you need to talk to him. We've discussed this already. It's no longer an option and it seems to me that no matter where you go, he'll always be behind you, waiting for that talk. You're stronger than you give yourself credit for, Lily, and you need to act like an adult and do the right thing."

I gulped because I knew everything she said was true. I knew it before I called her, but I needed to hear her say it.

"Thank you, Dr. Blakely."

"Baby steps, Lily. Baby steps."

I hung up, grabbed my purse, and banged on his door.

"You do realize that this is a quiet hotel, right?"

"Don't be like that with me," I said as I gave him an evil look and walked into his room.

I heard him chuckle.

"This is how this situation is going to work. I need an assistant for the photo shoots and since you're here, you're going to help me. After we're finished with work, then I will listen to what you have to say but, until then, and only then, there will be no talk of such."

"Your terms, eh?" he asked.

"Yep. My terms. You game?"

"Sure. I'm game."

"Okay." I nodded my head. "Now, I need to go to Central Park. Are you coming?"

"I'm right behind you, but I have one question. Have you eaten yet?"

"I had a muffin," I replied.

"A muffin isn't a meal. So let's go grab some lunch before we head to Central Park."

"I pay for my own," I said.

"Deal."

We walked until we saw Rumours Bar and Grill. As soon as we stepped inside, we were taken to a booth. Luke told me that he had to use the bathroom and that he'd be right back. I watched him walk away and couldn't help but stare at his fine ass – the one I was missing badly and I wasn't the only one staring at him. The waiter came over to take our drink order so I ordered Luke a beer and a margarita for myself.

"I ordered you a beer since you weren't here," I said.

"Thank you." He smiled as he picked up his menu. "What are you going to order?"

"I think I might get the Chicken BLT Wrap."

"That sounds good. I'm looking at the Prime Rib French Dip."

"Oh, that sounds delicious too. Shit, now I don't know what to get." My head was starting to hurt.

He looked at me and flashed his sexy smile. "Why don't you order what you were going to? I'll order the French dip and we can share it."

We used to do that all the time. He would order one thing. I'd order something else and then we'd split it. I didn't know if we should do that or not. Things between us were awkward and not normal, but what the hell, I really wanted to try that French dip.

"Okay."

After setting our drinks in front of us, the waiter took our order. The place was hopping and crowded with people. It was your typical bar with big screen TVs lining the walls and a different sports game on every one. Once my eyes finished scanning the place, they caught the attention of Luke, who was staring at me.

"Why are you staring at me?"

Suddenly, he held out his hand. "Hi, I'm Luke Matthews and you are?"

I narrowed my eyes at him as I cocked my head and a half smile fell across my lips. I stuck out my hand and placed it in his.

"I'm Lily Gilmore."

"It's nice to meet you, Lily Gilmore."

Our hands were still locked when the waiter brought our food. His touch, which I'd craved, was comforting and I found myself having a hard time letting go.

Chapter 29

Luke

Starting over. Reintroducing ourselves. I let go of her hand as soon as the waiter set down my plate in front of me. Her half smile, the look on her face; it was a start. Hopefully, the start of a new beginning for both of us. I picked up half of my sandwich and handed it to her. She picked up half of hers, and we exchanged.

"Thank you, Miss Gilmore."

"Thank you, Mr. Matthews."

"Why don't you tell me a little about what I'll be doing as your assistant?"

She explained about lighting and handing her different cameras and lenses. Just as long as I got to be with her, I didn't care what I did. As we were eating, her phone beeped with a message from Brynn. She quickly typed a message back and then looked at me.

"How are you now with Brynn and Hunter? Please don't get mad at me for bringing it up."

"I found that the universe works in mysterious ways. I met Hunter so he could get together with my sister if that makes sense. The two of them were meant to be together and I see that now."

"As in fate?" I asked.

She looked down as she dipped her French fry in ketchup. "Yeah. Maybe."

There was still a hint of pain in her response. "So then all is good with you and them?"

I was trying to get a feel for how she might or might not forgive me.

"Things are okay, but they will never go back to the way it used to be. I think the thing for me is how they kept it from me, how I almost married him, and how they would have still went on together behind my back. That will always be in the forefront of my mind."

Progress. She was talking to me the way she used to. She could have told me that it was none of my business, but instead, she chose to talk about it, which made me happy. We finished eating and we paid our own bill. I was going to have to respect her wishes if I wanted a second chance with her. I got up from the booth first and waited for her to get out before leaving the restaurant. As soon as she slid out from her seat, I placed my hand on the small of her back. We walked to Central Park and took in the beauty it had to offer. Lily had brought her camera and started taking pictures.

"Lily, look! It's the Central Park Zoo. Let's go," I excitedly said as I grabbed her hand without even thinking about it. "Sorry," I said as I looked down and let go of her hand. "I guess I got overly excited."

She didn't say a word. She just smiled. We each bought our own ticket and headed straight to the penguin exhibit. As we stood and watched them, the smile on Lily's face never left. She loved the penguins just as much as I did. Our next stop was the snow leopards.

"Look at how beautiful they are," she said as she took their pictures. "Did you know that their teeth are over four inches long?" she asked as she looked over at me.

"No, I didn't know that. I would hate to get caught in a mouth like that."

"I love their coloring. Did you know that their colors are so they can camouflage themselves in the mountains?"

"No," I said as I arched one eyebrow. "Are you a snow leopard expert and just never told me?"

She laughed. "No. I was obsessed with them one time when I was a child and I wanted a baby snow leopard as a pet. My dad told me to do a lot of research and write a paper on the facts about them and he'd take it under consideration. Let's just say that he was high when he said that and then denied he'd ever said it when he was sober."

"That was really shitty."

"Yeah, well, he was sometimes a shitty father."

She walked away from the snow leopards and went over to look at the lemurs.

"Look! It's King Julian!" She smiled.

"Is there anything special I should know about them?"

She laughed. "No. I never wanted one, but look at how cute they are. I may have to reconsider."

I looked around and noticed a stand that sold stuffed animals. I told Lily that I needed to find a restroom and that I'd be right back. I made my way to the stand that I noticed earlier that sold snow leopard stuffed animals. I purchased one and then found Lily taking pictures of the red pandas.

"I found something," I said.

"Really? What?"

I handed her the baby snow leopard with a smile. "He asked me if I knew your name because he wanted to go home with you."

She took the stuffed animal from my hands. "Luke," she said as she looked down.

"Now you have the baby snow leopard you always wanted. I thought since you did all that research, you deserved one."

"Thank you," she said as she held it up to her face and smiled.

****

Lily

Happy. That was how I was at the moment. He caught me off guard and I didn't know what to do.

"Are you okay?" he asked.

"I just have a headache. Come on; let's go see the other animals."

I really wasn't feeling well and after we looked at all the animals, we hailed a cab and took it back to the hotel. Luke put his hand on my forehead.

"Lily, you're burning up. I think you may have a fever."

"I don't think I have a fever. I'm just really tired. I think I'm still jet-lagged."

"You have a fever."

When we reached the hotel, Luke told me to go to my room and that he'd pick up some Motrin from the gift shop. I did as he asked because I didn't have the strength to argue with him. My headache was getting worse by the second. When I opened the door, I threw my purse on the floor, kicked off my shoes, threw myself on the bed, and closed my eyes. A few moments later, Luke knocked on the door. It took every bit of strength I had to get up and answer it.

"Come on. Let's get you into bed, Lily. Do you want to change first?"

I nodded as I lay down across the comforter. "In the top drawer is a pair of shorts and a tank top."

He handed them to me and I made my way to the bathroom to change. When I was done, Luke had the covers pulled back and I climbed in, laying my head on the soft pillow. He took the thermometer he purchased from the lobby shop and put it under my tongue.

"Keep it under there." He smiled as he gave me the snow leopard.

After a few minutes, the thermometer beeped and he took it from my mouth.

"Ouch. It's 102. I told you that you had a fever." He opened the Motrin bottle and handed me a bottle of water.

I took the little orange pills and chased them down with water. I couldn't believe that I was sick. I was never sick. This had to be the worst timing. I clutched my snow leopard tightly to my chest as Luke pulled the covers up over me.

"Get some rest," he said as he lightly put his hand on my head.

I just wanted to sleep. Thank God the photo shoot was the day after tomorrow. Hopefully, I'd be better by then. I remembered drifting off into a deep sleep, but at the same time, I felt restless because I had a dream about me and Luke. A dream where we were having sex and it was nothing short of incredible until I looked up and saw Callie staring down at us. My eyes flew open and I sat straight up, then I fell back down. Luke was sitting on the couch and he instantly came to my side.

"Are you okay?"

"Why are you still here?" I asked sleepily. "And, yeah, I just had a nightmare. It's probably the fever."

He went into the bathroom and wet a washcloth and then placed it across my forehead. "Feeling any better?"

"No," I replied as I looked at him. "You don't have to stay here. You can go. I appreciate everything you've already done."

"I came to New York to be with you, Lily, and you're sick. There's no way I'm leaving you when you're like this. Do you want to know what the best part is?"

"What?"

"You don't have the strength to argue with me." He smiled.

"You're right," I said as I closed my eyes and fell back asleep.

Once again, I woke up and looked over at Luke, who was lying across the couch, sleeping. I had to pee, so I climbed out of bed and made my way to the bathroom. My body felt like it had been hit by a train, with every muscle and joint in agony. As I was in the bathroom, there was a knock on the door.

"You okay in there, Lily?" Luke asked.

"Yeah," I said as I flushed the toilet.

I walked out of the bathroom and Luke was standing there with the bottle of Motrin in his hands.

"You need to take a couple more."

"How long have I been sleeping?" I asked as I climbed back into bed.

"Five hours."

"I want to take a bath."

"I'll start one for you and then I have something I have to do, but I'll be back."

I nodded my head, and after he started the water, I took off my shirt. He looked at me with hunger in his eyes. I wasn't even thinking straight and I shouldn't have done that in front of him.

"Is it okay if I take your room key?"

"Yeah. It's fine."

"Okay. I'm leaving, but I'll be back. Be careful in the bathtub. I won't be gone long."

I gave him a half smile and he left the room. Stripping out of the rest of my clothes, I climbed into the relaxing tub and closed my eyes.

Chapter 30

Luke

Seeing her sick like that really upset me. I'd never known Lily to be sick unless you count the nights she got drunk and was hanging over the toilet vomiting while I held back her hair. I had remembered seeing a deli earlier when Lily and I were walking down the street. As I stepped through the door, I could smell the aroma of chicken soup with a mix of pastrami.

"Can you I help you?" the girl behind the counter asked.

"I'd like to order a bowl of chicken noodle soup, a corned beef sandwich, and a tuna salad sandwich with lettuce and tomato."

"Coming right up, sir." She smiled.

Once my order was ready to go, I stopped into a party store before heading back to the hotel. I picked up a few bottles of water and a few bottles of Coke. I needed to make sure Lily stayed hydrated. When I opened the door, Lily walked out of the bathroom with her robe on.

"What did you get?" she asked as she slipped her feet into the complimentary slippers and climbed back into bed, sitting up against the headboard.

I set the brown bags down on the table and pulled out her soup and sandwich. "I brought you some chicken noodle soup and a sandwich. You need to eat."

"I'm not hungry."

"You don't need to eat the sandwich now, but the soup you do," I said as I handed it to her with a spoon. "I also picked up bottles of water and coke. It's way cheaper than what the hotel charges."

"Good thinking." She smiled.

I took my sandwich and sat down on the couch. Lily looked at me and I was surprised at what she said.

"You can sit on the bed. You don't need to sit all the way over there."

"Are you sure?"

"Yeah," she replied as she patted the bed.

I took my sandwich and sat up next to her.

"I want to thank you for taking care of me. This really would have sucked if I was alone."

I wanted to kiss her so badly, but I couldn't. One, she was sick and two, she wasn't ready. I could still sense the hesitance in her.

"You're welcome. You know that I'll always take care of you."

"Luke, don't," she said as she looked down.

"We're going to talk, Lily. Not tonight and maybe not tomorrow, but we're going to talk and you better be ready."

****

Lily

I told Luke to go to his room and get some sleep. I didn't want him staying in my room all night and sleeping on the couch. He paid a lot of money for his room and I wanted to make sure he was comfortable.

"Are you going to be okay?" he asked.

"I'll be fine. I'm already feeling a little bit better, thanks to you. Plus, I have Leo to keep me company."

"Who's Leo?" he asked with a confused look.

I held up the snow leopard and smiled.

"Ah, so that's his name. I'm taking your room key in case you need me in the middle of the night."

"That's fine. If I need anything, I'll text you. I promise."

He leaned over and kissed me on the head. "Sorry. It's a habit. Feel better and sleep well," he said as he got up from the bed and left the room. When the door shut, I regretted telling him to leave. I felt alone. I pulled out my phone and called Giselle to see how Isabella was doing. They were bringing her home from the hospital today.

"Lily. How are you?" she answered.

"Sick. Can you believe it?"

"Oh no. Flu?"

"I don't know. I have a fever and I'm really tired and achy all over."

"Make sure to stay hydrated."

"Luke is making sure of that."

"So lover boy found you?"

"Yep. He sure did."

"Are you being nice?"

I rolled my eyes. "Yes. He's taking such good care of me and it hurts," I said as a tear fell down my face.

"Why does it hurt? He loves you and you love him. Stop fighting it, Lily. Damn, I love you, but you are being dumb about this."

"You don't understand it, Giselle. I'm doing this for him."

"What? What the hell are you talking about?"

"Listen, I called to find out how Isabella is doing."

"She's fine. Now back to what you're doing for Luke."

"I have to go. I'm not feeling good. I'll call you later." *Click.*

I woke up the next morning to the smell of coffee and Luke sitting on the edge of my bed with his hand across my forehead. I opened one eye.

"What are you doing?"

"Checking to see if you still have a fever."

"Do I?"

"It doesn't feel like it, but we better take your temperature," he said as he stuck the thermometer under my tongue. "I brought you breakfast. I ordered room service for us and had it delivered to my room so you wouldn't be disturbed. I brought it over."

The thermometer beeped and Luke smiled as he read it. "99.5. I would say you're getting better."

I sat up with ease. My body didn't ache as bad as yesterday and my headache seemed to have disappeared. Luke set the tray on my lap and then climbed in next to me with his. I took a sip of coffee and it was so delicious. As I lifted the silver lid from the plate, I took in the aroma of bacon and eggs. I looked over at Luke and smiled.

"Good choice, Mr. Matthews."

"Did you sleep well?" he asked.

"I think so. I don't remember waking up at all."

"That's good. I think you're on the mend. You probably had some twelve- or twenty-four-hour bug."

I sat there and ate my eggs as a sudden thought came to mind. I turned and looked at him.

"Who's running the bar?"

He laughed. "Is that what you're thinking about?"

"For some strange reason, it just hit me."

"Maddie, Candi, and my parents are holding down the fort."

"You mentioned that Cody quit. May I ask why?" I said as I spread the strawberry jam across a piece of toast.

"She was hitting on me and I had to put a stop to it. I guess she felt that she couldn't work for me anymore."

"You said you were over me, yet you showed up here."

"I said a lot of things I didn't mean, Lily."

We were interrupted by the ringing sound of my phone. I reached over and grabbed it from the nightstand.

"Hey, Adalynn."

"Hi, Lily. I have bad news. The photo shoot has to be rescheduled for next month."

"What? Why?"

"The damn designer didn't get the complete outfits done in time. Something about his sick mother. I don't know. But anyway, he was supposed to have overnighted them yesterday to the hotel, but how could he if he didn't finish them up? He was afraid to call me to tell me he was running behind."

"That's too bad."

"Tell me about it. But you stay the rest of the week and enjoy New York. Do me a favor and scout out some different locations for the shoot. You're creative and I know you'll find something amazing."

"Thanks, Adalynn. I'll talk to you soon." I hung up and sighed.

"What was that about?" Luke asked.

"The photo shoot isn't happening now until next month. She told me to stay the rest of the week and scout out some locations."

"That's too bad," he said.

"Yeah. But on the bright side, I get to come back. Isn't that right, Leo?" I said as I kissed my snow leopard's face.

Chapter 31

Luke

We finished eating breakfast and I took the trays over to the table. I happened to look out the window and noticed it was raining.

"It's raining."

"Rain? What's that?" Lily laughed.

"Yeah, no kidding. It's been quite a while since California has seen some."

Now that the photo shoot was cancelled, I wondered if it was the right time for our talk. I really needed to do this because I was desperate for her. Even though things between us the past day had been amazing, we needed to talk. I walked over to the bed and grabbed her hand. She knew exactly what I was doing because she had a look of fear in her eyes.

"Babe, we need to talk and we need to do it now."

She took in a sharp breath and pulled her hand away. "I know."

"That night was a shock for both of us and I'm not proud of how I handled myself. I never should have walked out on you and I'm so sorry. I want to erase that night and start over."

"You never should have left me." She started to cry. "You should have stayed and we could have talked about it. I was in just as much shock as you and you didn't love me enough to stay. You walked out on me like everyone else in my life!" she yelled as she pointed her finger at me.

"Lily, I'm so sorry. You also need to understand what seeing that picture meant. What I felt. The things going through my head. To think that we'd actually had a conversation before you moved to Santa Monica, and that we looked into each other's eyes before we even knew each other's names is extraordinary. Lily, you were meant to be in my life, starting from the day you walked over to my table."

****

Lily

Oh God. I couldn't do this. I didn't know what to say; my throat felt like it was closing. He was broken right now, but he would heal. When he didn't have to see me anymore, he'd heal. I started to shake and my breathing became constricted. I threw on a pair of yoga pants and a sweat shirt.

"Lily, what are you doing?"

"I can't do this."

"What do you mean?" he yelled.

I threw open my suitcase and dug for my tennis shoes. When I found them, I forced my feet into them as quickly as I could and I grabbed my purse.

"I'm sorry, Luke. I promise you'll be okay," I cried as I flew out of the hotel room.

The elevator doors were open because a young couple had just stepped on. My face was soaked in tears and my nose was running. The pretty brunette looked at me and handed me a tissue.

"Thanks," I cried.

The doors opened and I ran. I ran through the lobby and out onto the soaking wet streets of New York City. I could see Central Park. *He'll be okay. He'll be okay*, I kept chanting over and over again. I figured if I said it enough, in time I would believe it. The rain was pouring from the sky and I was soaked, as were the people leaving the park and trying to seek shelter.

"Lily!" I heard Luke yell. "You can't do this. You can't just walk away from me. I love you and I refuse to live without you."

I stopped in the middle of the grass. "You don't understand!" I screamed as I turned around and looked at him. He was soaked, standing there, looking at me like a lost soul.

"Make me understand because I don't know who the hell you've become. I love you and I know damn well you love me. You're still in love with me, right?"

I turned away and closed my eyes. If I told him no, I'd be lying because I loved him more than my own life.

"Lily, answer me!" he yelled as he walked up to me. He grabbed my arms. "Are you still in love with me?"

I broke out of his grip. "Yes. Yes, I love you and I am in love with you. But it's too late; we can't ever be together. We can't go back to how things used to be."

"Why? What the hell is your problem?"

I wiped the rain from my forehead as I stood there soaking wet, crying and shaking, not only from the cold, but from my own fears.

"Make me understand," he cried.

"I gave you the tickets. You had a great time, a time you didn't think would be your last with her. You were broken, so broken after her death and then I came along and put you back together. You didn't know that I was the girl who gave you the tickets. I didn't even know I was the girl. I didn't remember you. How could I? I was in my own turmoil of my fucked up life and when I saw you and Callie holding hands and smiling at that table, I knew you were the perfect couple and I wanted something good to come out of the hell I was trying to climb out of. But instead, my hell turned into your hell, and I will never forgive myself for that, and every time you look at me, you're going to be reminded of how I was the one. It will always be in the back of your mind that I was responsible for Callie's death, especially when you see or hear something that reminds you of her. I can't live the rest of my life causing you any more pain. Don't you get it? I caused you pain before we even met."

He stood there, crying as he stared at me. "You're wrong, babe. I don't blame you. I'm so sorry that I even said that. I didn't mean it. I was in shock. You don't cause me any pain and I don't think about that when I look at you. All I see when I look at you is my soul-mate and my best friend. The girl that rescued me and fell in love with me. The girl who I love so damn much that I would give up my life for. Lily, don't do this to us. Don't do this to me. You stand there and talk about causing me pain. The only pain you'll cause me is if you walk away from me."

I stepped closer to him and placed my hand on his cheek. "I can't. You'll move on and you'll find someone who will love you just as much as I do. I'm doing this for you. You have to understand that."

"No! I will never understand your reasoning. Congratulations, Lily, you just caused me the worst kind of pain imaginable. Have a great life," he said as he turned around and walked away.

As I watched him, I fell to my knees, sobbing and wanting to run after him. What was I doing? Did I even know anymore? I couldn't think or see straight as I made my way out of Central Park. I was walking down the streets, dazed and confused and crying. He said that he'd give up his life for me, but what he didn't understand was that I was doing that for him. I was giving up my life for him.

After walking for what seemed like hours, a man called out to me.

"You're welcome to use my umbrella, miss."

I looked over in between the two buildings and saw a homeless man seeking shelter under a large overhang. He was sitting on the ground, looking up at me. His clothes were tattered and worn. He wore a tan-colored coat and had the hood up, covering his head. I could see the dirt spots on his face and fingers. He was older, I would say in his fifties. I stopped because this man who looked like he had nothing had offered me his umbrella.

"Thank you," I said as I took it from him and sat down on the cold wet ground.

"You look pretty beaten up. I haven't seen you around here before."

"I'm not from here. I live in California."

"Ah, California. I was there once. Beautiful place, but holds a lot of bad memories for me. The name's Philip." He smiled.

"I'm Lily," I said as I held out my hand.

He looked at me strangely, like he was unsure, and then he slowly placed his hand in mine and shook it. "You don't mind shaking hands with a homeless man?"

"No. You may be homeless, but you're still a person."

He looked away. "That's probably the nicest thing anyone has said to me in a very long time. It's nice to meet you, Lily."

The rain started to slow down, and I was so cold. My problems seemed far and few compared to Philip's.

"I saw a little diner around the corner. Are you hungry? I really need some coffee."

"That's sweet of you, Lily, but you don't want to be seen with a homeless man. I'm fine."

"You offered me the use of your umbrella and I want to thank you. So come on, Philip, let's go sit in the diner, have some coffee, something to eat, and dry off."

"You're serious, aren't you?" he asked.

"Yeah. I very serious." I smiled.

"Well, if you insist. Who am I to turn down such a generous offer from a beautiful girl?"

We both stood up and walked around the corner. When we stepped into the diner and I told the hostess we would like a booth, she gave me a strange look and then showed us to the only booth that was available.

"Excuse me, miss. Are you okay?"

"I'm fine," I replied as I looked at her strangely.

"I'm sorry," she said as she walked away.

I looked at Philip and he laughed. "People are strange. Just ignore her."

Chapter 32

Luke

I went back to the hotel and, as soon as I got to my room, I stepped into the hot shower. I placed my hands against the smooth, tiled wall and cried. I completely broken down. My head was spinning and reeling with all kinds of emotions. How could she do this to us? She said she still loved me, yet we couldn't be together. She was wrong. Dead wrong! I would never look at her and think of Callie. She made her decision and there was nothing that I could do to change it. I'd tried and I couldn't do it anymore. When I got back to California, I was moving out of the apartment building. I couldn't be near her. She was so fucking worried about me feeling pain every time I looked at her. Well, she was right. Now I would because I loved her, and it hurt way too much to look at her and know that I couldn't have her.

After I finished my shower, I looked up flights back home. The next flight out of New York was at nine o'clock tonight. FUCK! I needed something earlier, but I was out of luck. I put on some dry clothes and lay down on the bed. I replayed our conversation over and over again until I fell asleep.

****

Lily

"Order anything and as much as you want," I said to Philip.

"If you'll excuse me, Lily, I'm going to use the restroom and clean myself up a little."

I smiled as he got up from the booth. The waitress came by and poured coffee in both of our cups. A few moments later, Philip walked back to the table, looking better. He had washed his face and hands, making himself look cleaner. He sat down, and when he took a sip of his coffee, he closed his eyes as if it was the best thing he'd ever tasted.

"The aroma of coffee always gets me. I love it."

"Me too."

There was something about Philip that reminded me of my father. I couldn't exactly put my finger on it, but there was something about him that comforted me.

"When I first saw you, you looked like you had been crying. Would you like to talk about what happened?"

"Not really," I replied.

"Sometimes talking to a complete stranger is more therapeutic than talking to a friend or someone who knows you. They just seem to tell you what you want to hear."

I smiled at him as I took a sip of my coffee. The waitress walked over and placed our food in front of us. As we ate, I told him everything, starting from my wedding day. He sat there and intently listened to me as I told him all about Luke, but he never spoke a word. He just listened and now it was his turn.

"So why are you homeless?" I asked.

"Getting right down to the nitty gritty, I see." He smiled.

"Sorry," I said as I looked down. "You said that California held a lot of bad memories for you."

He took in a deep breath. "I had it all once. A high-paying job, a beautiful wife, two beautiful children, a dog, and the house with the white picket fence, until my wife was killed in a car accident three years ago."

"I'm so sorry," I said.

"We were having a dinner party that evening and she had asked me if I would stop on the way home from the office and pick up some extra bottles of wine. I had a crazy and bad day and I forgot. When I got home, I wasn't in the best of moods and I wasn't looking forward to having people over. Elise asked me where the wine was and I told her that I had a bad day and I forgot to stop and pick some up. She told me to go back out and go buy some. After saying a few choice words to her, I told that I would after I took a shower and changed. She could sense the irritation in my voice, so she told me to forget it and she grabbed the keys from the counter and went herself. After I took a shower and got dressed, she still wasn't home. An hour and a half had passed and I started to worry. Her cell phone went straight to voicemail every time I called. Our dinner guests were scheduled to arrive in an hour and this wasn't like Elise to be gone so long. That was when I climbed into my vehicle and drove to the party store where we get all our liquor. As I was close, I noticed a long back-up of cars. If she was in that lineup, she would have called to let me know. I sat there for fifteen minutes without moving until I got out of my car and saw flashing red lights up ahead. I walked in between the cars to get a closer look. It had looked like an accident happened. My heart stopped beating when I saw a car that looked just like Elise's completely smashed. I asked God to please not let it be her, but when I got closer, I looked at the license plate, and it was her car. I looked over next to the car and saw someone covered in a white sheet. As I started screaming her name, two police officers ran up to me and held me back. They said that she was already dead when they got there. Apparently, she was going through a green light and a semi-truck driver didn't realize the light was red on his side and he just went through and smashed into her."

A tear fell down his cheek as several fell down mine. I reached over and grabbed his hand. "I am so sorry that happened to you. That wasn't your fault."

He looked down as he continued eating. "That was as much my fault as it was the truck driver's. If I never would have forgotten to get the wine on the way home or argued with her about it, she wouldn't have gone herself and she'd still be here today."

I was in complete shock by his story. "Philip. That was not your fault. We can spend a lifetime doing the 'what ifs' and it won't change anything."

"Just like Callie's accident?" he asked.

I instantly changed the subject. "What about your children? Where are they?"

"My mom is taking care of them."

"I'm sorry to ask this, but how could you just leave your kids like that after they lost their mother?"

He gently smiled at me as he placed his hand on mine. "I was a constant reminder of their mother's death. They overheard us arguing that day. They heard the things she was saying to me. The way she called me lazy and selfish and never thought about anybody but myself. They told me flat out that she would still be alive if I had only done what she had asked and they were right. I told my mom that I was going on a trip and to look after the kids. That was three years ago and I never looked back," he said as he stared off in a daze. "Every time I looked into my children's eyes, I would see the blame. It was too much to handle, so I had to spare them."

I sat there and was at a loss for words. "So you gave up everything? Why?"

"Because, my dear, I gave up on me. I lost all my self-worth, dignity, clarity. I realize now that I was a fool and I was wrong. Nothing's really as it seems. Your perception is the one thing that pixels the truth. I didn't cause my wife's death, just like you didn't cause Callie's, and I can guarantee that Luke won't ever look at you and see you as the woman who was responsible. I just wish that I could be with my children again and make them understand."

"You can. It's not too late," I said as I squeezed his hand.

"It is; for me, at least." He smiled.

"No. No it's not. We can call your children right now. You can talk to them and I'll send you home. You can fly back to California with me. What's your mom's number? I can call her for you and then you can talk to your children."

He rattled off his mother's phone number as I punched it into my phone. As it was ringing, he got up from the booth and placed his hand on my shoulder.

"Take what I've told you today and rebuild your relationship. Clear your mind and see the truth for what it really is, not what you think it is. Second chances are always the best in life, Lily." He smiled.

Philip turned, walked through the diner, and out the door. Before I had the chance to stop him, I heard an older woman's voice on the other end of the phone.

"Hello," she answered.

"Hi, my name is Lily Gilmore and I'm calling about your son, Philip."

"Yes. How can I help you?"

"He's in New York and we just had a long conversation and—"

"Excuse me. Is this some kind of a joke? My son, Philip, passed away a year ago from pneumonia."

My face dropped and I sat there in silence, looking at the door. "I'm so sorry. Maybe I have the wrong number. I'm so sorry." *Click.*

What the fuck just happened? The waitress came by and put her hand on my arm.

"Are you okay, sweetie? You look like you've just seen a ghost."

"That man that was sitting here with me for the last four hours."

"What man, sweetie?"

"What do you mean 'what man'? You served him food."

"No. You've been the only one sitting here for the last four hours. Do you need me to call someone for you?"

I heard his voice in my head as I stared straight ahead where he sat. *"Clear your mind and see the truth for what it really is, not what you think it is."*

"I'm fine. I'm just really tired. Here," I said as I pulled out my money and handed it to her. "Keep the change. I need to go."

"Thank you, sweetie. Take care of yourself," she yelled as I quickly left the diner.

Chapter 33

Luke

As I sat on the edge of the bed with my feet planted firmly on the floor, I sighed as I cupped my face in my hands. I picked up my phone and there were no messages. I shook my head as I got up and threw my things in the suitcase. I had slept a little too long and I needed to get to the airport. After quickly scanning the room and making sure I had everything, I went down to the lobby and checked out. I couldn't get out of here fast enough. The valet hailed a cab for me and told the driver to take me to the airport. Since I still had a little bit of time, I decided to get something to eat before heading to my gate. I pulled my phone from my pocket and dialed Sam.

"Hey, bro. Gretchen and I were just talking about you and Lily. How are the two of you? Getting along, I hope."

"It's over for good, man. She decided it, not me."

"Luke, I'm sorry. I'm going to put you on speaker so Gretchen can hear."

"Luke, what the fuck happened? What did she say to you?" Gretchen asked.

"She said that if we were together and that every time I looked at her, I would be reminded of Callie. She said that she caused me enough pain in my life and she couldn't do it anymore." My eyes started to fill with tears.

"She's an idiot!" Gretchen yelled. "What the hell is the matter with her and her fucked up way of thinking? That's what she meant that night at Charley's birthday party. I told her that you're so in love with her and she said that you only think you are."

I shook my head as I took a bite of my pizza. This was unreal to me. "I'm at the airport now. My flight will be boarding soon. I'll talk to you guys later."

"Take care, Luke, and we're on your side," Sam said.

I finished my pizza and then headed to my gate. I really thought that we'd be flying home together. I was dead wrong. My phone had ten percent battery left, so I turned it off and put it back in my pocket. As I sat down in the chair, I noticed the couple sitting across me. They were smiling, holding hands, and sharing small kisses. I couldn't take sitting there, so I moved to the other side and sat in the corner.

****

Lily

Shit. I didn't really know where I was. When I walked here from Central Park, I was in such a daze of confusion, that I didn't pay attention. I hailed a cab and told him to step on it to the Trump Hotel. He looked at me strangely until I held out a twenty-dollar bill.

"It's a matter of life and death. I need to get there NOW!"

"Sure thing, lady."

He pulled out into traffic. Weaving in and out, slamming on the brakes, and almost getting me killed a few times. He pulled up to the Trump and the valet opened the door. I paid my fare and ran into the hotel, pressing the button on the elevator numerous times. The doors finally opened and I rode it up to my floor, with a few stops on the way up. I pushed my way through the crowd of people on the elevator when the doors opened and went right to Luke's room. I knocked on the door and then called his name. No answer. I knocked again. No answer. I BANGED on it. No answer. I pulled my phone from my purse and dialed his number; it went straight to voicemail. SHIT.

I got out my room key, went inside, changed into different clothes, and went down to the front desk.

"Can I help you, miss?"

"I'm trying to get a hold of Luke Matthews in room 2212 and he's not answering and I'm worried."

"Mr. Matthews already checked out."

"Oh." My heart sank. "That's right; he said something about going home earlier than planned. He was going home, right?"

"I don't know, miss. He didn't say."

"Right. Thank you."

I turned around and my eyes filled with tears. What was I going to do now? I tried to call him again and it went straight to voicemail. As I walked outside the hotel, I asked the valet about Luke and I showed him his picture. He told me that he took a cab to the airport about an hour ago. I thanked him as I hopped in a cab and told the driver to take me to the airport. I searched flights out of LaGuardia and the only flight that Luke would have been on was the nine o'clock flight. I looked at my watch. I still had time. I could make it.

"Excuse me, but you need to drive faster," I said to the cab driver.

"Ma'am, this is New York. I'm doing the best I can."

We finally reached the airport and I ran to security and was instantly stopped.

"Boarding pass, please."

"I'm not flying out. I need to go and get my boyfriend. I need to tell him how much I love him and that I made a terrible mistake."

He looked at me with irritation. "You aren't getting through security if you don't have a boarding pass."

"Have you ever been in love?" I asked.

"No," he said as he made me turn around and pointed to the ticket counter.

"I can see why," I mumbled as I stood in line.

I was running out of time. I needed to get to the front of the line so I could buy a ticket and try to stop Luke. I couldn't let him get on that plane. I walked up front to the next person in line. A young man. Actually, a very cute young man.

"Excuse me. I don't have time to stand in line. I need to get to my boyfriend before he boards his plane. Can I please have your spot in line?"

"Sorry, lady, but I'm in a hurry too."

I flashed a fifty-dollar bill at him. "Still in a hurry?"

"One more person won't make a difference," he said as he took the money from my hand and motioned for me to get in front of him. I looked back at him. "I want you know that your cuteness factor just went out the window."

"Next," the man at the counter said.

"I need a ticket."

"To where?"

"I don't care where. Just give me a ticket!"

He looked at me and narrowed his eyes. "You don't know where you're going?"

"Fine. Give me a ticket for the next flight out to LAX."

"Okay. That flight leaves at one a.m."

"Wait. Don't you have a nine o'clock flight?"

"Yes, but that's sold out."

I sighed. "Fine, give me the one o'clock. Just hurry," I said as I handed him my I.D. and credit card.

"Here you go. Do you have any bags to check?"

"No. I don't," I said as I grabbed the ticket and ran to security.

"I see you're going on a trip." The security officer smiled.

I shot him a look as I waited to go through. It was all moving pretty fast, but his plane was boarding right as of this minute. I took off my shoes, threw them in the bin, got scanned, and grabbed them as I stood and looked at the monitor to find out which gate he was at. Once I found out, I looked at the signs and, oh shit, I had to run. Of course his gate would be at the other end. I ran through the airport, pushing people, saying excuse me and almost tripping over someone's cane. I was going to tell Luke how wrong I was and beg him for his forgiveness. Why was I so stupid? How was I so stupid? I didn't have time to analyze my stupidity as I finally reached his gate and the doors shut. I ran up to the desk.

"I need to get on that plane."

"I'm sorry, miss, but it's too late; it's closed."

"No, no. You don't understand. My life is hanging by a thread and the answer to that is on that plane. I need to get on that plane," I said with a shaky voice as I showed her my boarding pass.

She looked at me and raised her eyebrow. "Your ticket isn't even for this flight. Do you need us to call someone for you?"

Why does everyone keep asking me that? "No. I'm sorry," I replied as I looked down and slowly walked away.

I went to the window and looked out at the plane as the tears started to fall. I wasn't feeling well and it was the overwhelming sickness that I might never be with him again.

Chapter 34

Lily

I sat down in the chair for a moment to compose myself. Everything that had happened today was strange. I couldn't wrap my head around it. Did I even want to? I took in a deep breath and got up from the chair. I started to walk away when I heard my name from a distance.

"Lily?"

I stopped for a moment and turned around to find Luke standing a few feet in front of me. I ran to him and threw my arms around him as tight as I could.

"Oh my God, I'm so sorry for everything. Why are you here? You were on the plane!"

He looked confused but happy at the same time. "We have to switch planes. This one was having mechanical issues. Do you believe it?"

"Yes. After today, I do believe it. I believe everything, including you. I'm so sorry, Luke. Please forgive me. I love you so much and I can't lose you."

He grabbed my face and smashed his lips against mine. "Lily, you don't know how happy I am to hear you say that."

"Yes, I do. I love you.

"I love you too, babe. God, I can't believe this." He smiled as he picked me up and spun me around. "What happened? Why did you change your mind?"

"We can talk about that later. Let's go back to the hotel. We have so much to catch up on."

"We sure do, babe. We sure do."

****

Luke

We couldn't keep our hands off of each other. She felt warm again. She fumbled in her purse for the keycard as I had her up against the door, passionately kissing her. She handed me the card and I inserted it as the green light flashed and I turned the knob.

"Wait," I said as I broke our kiss.

I held the door open with my foot and I picked her up and carried her inside. She smiled as her arms were wrapped around my neck.

"Babe, I want to make love to you so bad. But we have to take your temperature first."

"What?!" she exclaimed.

"You feel really warm."

She sighed as I sat her down on the bed. "Fine," she said as she stuck the thermometer in her mouth. It beeped. She looked at it and then at me.

"It's 100.5 and I don't care because we already mixed saliva, so you're going to get it anyway." She smiled as she pulled me down on top of her.

"I didn't say I wasn't going to make love to you. I was just saying you felt warm."

My lips trailed her neck as she fumbled with the button on my jeans. Once she managed to get them unbuttoned, she unzipped the zipper and stuck her hand down the front of my pants. I moaned.

"You have no idea how much I've missed this," she gasped.

"Kind of like I missed these." I smiled as my hand grabbed her breast.

Her hand was stroking me up and down and I felt like I was already going to come. I stood up, kicked off my shoes, and stripped out of my clothes. Lily sat up and did the same, except for her bra. She left that on and smiled at me. She knew how much I loved to take it off of her. I climbed on the bed behind her as she sat straight up. My tongue made tiny circles around her shoulders and upper back as my hands unhooked her bra. I reached in front of her and lightly took hold of both her breasts, kneading them and pinching her hard nipples. Her moans increased as she placed her hands on mine, guiding my hands around her breasts.

"God, I love you, Lily."

"I love you, Luke."

She turned around so she was facing me and sat up on her knees. My hand found its way in between her legs as my fingers plunged inside her and my thumb slowly rubbed her clit. She arched her back and started making the "ah" sounds as she ran her fingers through my hair.

"You're so wet. I think you need to be wetter, though," I said as I brought my mouth down to her. My tongue softly circling around her swollen area was arousing her even more. She began to thrust her hips as my tongue dipped inside of her and played around.

"Oh God, Luke. Baby, what are you doing to me?" she asked with bated breath.

"Making you come," I whispered as my tongue circled her clit and my fingers went inside her. I brought her to the edge and smiled as she released herself on me.

She pushed me back and climbed on top, but not before sucking me off for a few minutes. Her mouth wrapped around my cock was the hottest thing to me. I loved watching her. She brought her lips to mine and gently climbed on top of me. I was so hard and more than ready to be inside of her. She lowered herself onto me and began slowly moving. Looking at her full naked body making love to me was amazing. Our lips were locked tight as I thrust myself inside her. We both gasped as I nipped her bottom lip. She broke our kiss and her lips traveled from my chin down to my nipples. She licked each one before sitting up and moving her hips in a circular motion. I couldn't get enough of her. She felt so good.

"Lily, you feel amazing."

"So do you. You're so hard," she said as she leaned back and placed her hands on my legs.

I grabbed a hold of her hips and moved her back and forth on my cock. She was swelling and getting ready to have orgasm number two.

"You're so warm inside. Lily, I'm going to come."

"Me too!" she yelled.

She sat straight up and rode me faster as her legs tightened at my side and we both came at the same time, calling out each other's names. She collapsed on top of me and hugged me tight. Our hearts beat rapidly together as our breathing began to slow. My hands traveled softly up and down her naked back. It felt so good to have her body near mine again.

"You need to take some Motrin," I whispered in her ear.

She let out a laugh as she rolled off of me. "Really, Luke?"

"Yeah, babe. Really." I winked.

Chapter 35

Lily

I took some Motrin like Luke said I had to and got up from the bed.

"Where are you going?" he asked.

"To get the room service menu. I'm starving." I smiled.

"Me too."

Luke climbed under the covers and I climbed in next to him as we looked over the menu.

"What time is it?" I asked.

He glanced over at the clock. It's eleven-thirty."

"Oh, well, then we need to be looking at the overnight dining menu."

"I think I want the burger."

"Me too." I smiled as I kissed his lips.

After I placed our order, I snuggled against Luke's chest as he stroked my hair.

"Lily, what made you change your mind about us?"

I slowly closed my eyes. *Do I tell him? Do I lie because I don't want him to think I'm crazy?*

"If I tell you, then you'll think I'm crazy and I mean certifiably legit crazy."

He chuckled as he kissed my head. "I would never think that."

I sat up, took in a deep breath, and told him all about Philip. "And as I was calling his mom, he got up from his seat and I'll never forget what he said to me."

"What did he say, babe?"

"He said, 'Take what I've told you today and rebuild your relationship. Clear your mind and see the truth for what it really is, not what you think it is. Second chances are always the best in life.' Then he walked away and when his mom answered, she told me that he had died a year ago of pneumonia."

"Are you serious? Lily, that's an amazing story."

"You don't think I'm crazy?"

"No. I don't. Think of all the events that happened involving us. Hunter and Brynn, the tickets, the accident, you moving in next door, our friends hooking up and getting together, you meeting Philip, and my plane having mechanical problems." He smiled. "Think about it, Lily; we were meant to be together, probably since the day we were born. I think we are the true meaning of soul mates."

He was right. If you put everything together like a puzzle, it all fit neatly together. Every event that we endured and every person that crossed our paths played a significant role in our lives. Once you link everything together, it all made sense.

Room service arrived and I quickly put on my robe as Luke pulled on his jeans and opened the door. The man wheeled the cart in, set up the table, and Luke tipped him before he left. We ate our burgers, talked, laughed, and made love two more times before going to sleep.

****

Luke

Waking up with Lily wrapped up in my arms was something that I missed so badly. I placed my hand across her forehead. She felt a little warm, but not as warm as last night.

"Are you checking me for a fever again?" she mumbled.

"Yes," I said as I pressed my lips against her forehead.

"What do you lips say?"

"They say I love you."

A smile graced her face as she opened her eyes and looked at me.

"And I love you."

"Why don't we take a shower, get dressed, grab some breakfast, and then go for a walk. I have someplace I want to take you."

"You forgot something."

"What?" I asked in confusion.

"You forgot to say that we had to make love."

"Oh, believe me, babe, I didn't forget that."

We climbed out of bed, took our shower, made love, got dressed, and then headed downstairs to eat. Once we finished breakfast, I took Lily's hand and we headed towards the place I couldn't wait to take her to. Once we stepped outside, I stopped and looked at her.

"If you're feeling up to it, we can walk. It'll take about fourteen minutes to get there. If you'd rather cab it, we can do that. It's up to you, babe."

"I want to walk. It's a pretty nice day out and we can explore the city."

We walked and did a lot of window shopping. Lily was so happy and so was I. My phone beeped with a text message from Sam.

"Dude, I thought you were getting in last night."

"Sorry, I forgot to tell you that the flight was rescheduled due to mechanical problems."

"When are you flying out?"

"I'll let you know."

We were coming up to the store I wanted to take Lily to, so I started to slow down. She looked at me.

"Why are you slowing down?"

"This is the store I wanted to go into with you."

She looked up and then at me. "Luke, this is Tiffany's."

I smiled as I led her inside. "Why are we here?" she asked.

"Lily," I said as I took hold of both her hands. "When I lost you, my world ended. My heart stopped beating and I felt like I was dead. You are the most important thing in my life and my world. I would die for you. I never want to lose you again and I want to spend the rest of my life with you. You're my soul mate and I love you so damn much. Will you marry me, Lily Gilmore?"

A tear fell from her eye as she brought her shaking hand to her mouth. "Yes. Yes. Of course I'll marry you, Luke." She smiled as she wrapped her arms around me.

I picked her up and twirled her around as the customers and employees clapped and whistled for us.

"Let's pick out your ring. I wanted us to pick one out together."

"What did I ever do to deserve someone like you?" she asked as she kissed me.

Chapter 36

Lily

All the rings were stunning, but I found one that Luke and I both loved. We both knew right away when I tried it on that it was the one because it fit perfectly, just like we did. I was the happiest person in the world and I couldn't wait to tell everyone that we were getting married.

"I have an idea. Let's send a mass video of us telling everyone that we're engaged."

"That's a great idea. Who's going to take it, though?"

"We'll find someone in Central Park. Let's do it there.

Luke loved the idea and we walked to Central Park. We walked over by the fountain and saw a young girl sitting by herself.

"Excuse me. Would you mind taking a video of me and my fiancé?"

"Not at all." She smiled.

I set the phone to video mode and Luke and I took our place in front of the fountain.

"Go," the young girl said.

"Hi, friends and family." I waved.

"Hey, everyone." Luke waved.

"We're sending you this video because we're going to stay in New York for a while longer. We have some news we wanted to share with you. I love this man so much!" I said as I pointed to Luke.

"And I love this woman so much!" he said as he pointed to me.

"And guess what? We're getting married!" we both said at the same time as I held up my hand with my ring on it.

"We love you all and we'll be home soon! Bye."

"Bye." Luke waved.

"Oh my God, that is so awesome!" the young girl said as she handed me my phone. "Congrats to you!"

"Thank you."

She walked away and we sent the video to all of our family and friends. We took a seat on a bench by the fountain and Luke took hold of my hand and brought it up to his lips.

"There are two sides of love; the upside and the downside. We've experienced both sides and I don't ever want to see the downside again. From here on out, babe, this is what the upside of love is. Us. Together forever. Loving each other no matter what life throws our way."

I brushed my lips against his. "You are the upside of love, Luke Matthews."

It wasn't long before our little moment was interrupted by both of our phones blowing up. We looked at each other and laughed as we turned them off and spent the rest of the week exploring New York and making up for lost time.

****

Two weeks later

"Give me my goddaughter." I smiled as Giselle and Lucky strolled into the bar.

"She's not just your goddaughter, don't forget." Gretchen smiled as she leaned down and kissed Isabella's head.

"I know that, but I will be her favorite godmother." I winked.

Gretchen laughed and put her arm around me. "I'm so excited to watch the boys play. It seems like it's been forever. What song are they doing?" Gretchen asked.

"I don't know. Luke wouldn't tell me. I tried to threaten him with no sex, but all he had to do was smile and I was on top of him."

"I am so happy for the both of you. I knew you'd come to your senses eventually. You said you'd tell us what happened to make you change your mind," Giselle said.

"I will, but not tonight. It's a long story."

Luke's dad took over Cody's position on a part-time basis and I couldn't have been happier. Luke and I both agreed to wait about a year before getting married. I wanted to make sure that my career and the studio were off the ground and running, and Luke wanted to make sure things stayed calm at the bar.

Neither one of us was going anywhere and we wanted time to plan the perfect wedding. I told Luke he was in charge of it since I'd already done it once before. He laughed and said that he'd gladly accept the challenge. Charley was so happy about the wedding that she wouldn't stop talking about it at Annie and Tom's house the other night. Lucky officially moved into Giselle's house and they became an exclusive couple. Gretchen didn't know this yet, but Sam bought her a ring and was going to propose to her on her birthday next month. Maddie and Adam were very much in love and Charley told us that her dad started staying the night. I bet you're wondering about my sister and Hunter. Well, they're getting married in a couple of months and Luke and I are attending the wedding. According to him, we need to go celebrate the couple that brought us together.

Luke walked over to me and kissed Isabella on the cheek. "You're turning me on holding that baby." He winked.

I smiled as he walked to the stage. The bar was packed and it seemed like more people came when they heard that Luke's band was playing. Luke picked up his guitar and he winked at me as he started to play "Don't Fear the Reaper."

"Oh, I love this song," Gretchen said as she began dancing to it. "I always wondered what it was about."

"It's about eternal love." I smiled as I walked towards the front of the stage and watched the love of my life sing to me.

This was without a doubt the upside of love, and I was loving every second of it.

About The Author

Sandi Lynn is a New York Times, USA Today and Wall Street Journal bestselling author who spends all of her days writing. She published her first novel, Forever Black, in February 2013. Her addictions are shopping, romance novels, coffee, chocolate, margaritas, and giving readers an escape to another world.

Please come connect with her at:

www.facebook.com/Sandi.Lynn.Author

www.twitter.com/SandilynnWriter

www.authorsandilynn.com

www.pinterest.com/sandilynnWriter

www.instagram.com/sandilynnauthor

https://www.goodreads.com/author/show/6089757.Sandi_Lynn

Playlist

Inside Your Heaven ~ Carrie Underwood

As It Seems ~ Lily Kershaw

Peace ~ O.A.R.

The Mess I Made ~ Parachute

Better In Time ~ Leona Lewis

Heal ~ Tom ODell

Nothing Left To Lose ~ Mat Kearney

Chandelier ~ Sia

(Don't Fear) The Reaper ~ Blue Oyster Cult

Love Remains The Same ~ Gavin Rossdale

Our Story ~ Graham Colton

Tomorrow Is A Long Time ~ Nickel Creek

(Everything I Do) I Do It For You ~ Bryan Adams

8273728R00139

Printed in Great Britain
by Amazon.co.uk, Ltd.,
Marston Gate.